CW00688670

This book is published by
Grosvenor House Publishing Ltd
Link House
140 The Broadway, Tolworth, Surrey, KT6 7HT.
www.grosvenorhousepublishing.co.uk

A CIP record for this book
is available from the British Library

ISBN 978-1-80381-452-0

High Heights

Thank you :)

J Ruth
28-Aug-23

by

J. Ruth

I write this at the end of my life.

Saying that, although I am confident that I can end my biological state of living by an act of will alone, of course, I haven't yet tried. If I cannot do it, if I am not able or willing, then there is no sign that I am any closer to the end of my life than I was yesterday, or on any of the uncountable days that came before that. But I see no reason that I should fail. There is no fear, no regret. I have the will.

And so I write this as I approach the end of my supernaturally long life. And what I want to tell you about now concerns a short passage of time, long ago, when I was not quite even one thousand years of age.

At that time I was living in a forest, although it was not a real forest. Not real in the sense that I then still meant the word. The trees stood in uniform lines, each trunk identical to the others, each configuration of branches and leaves identical to its neighbour. For, as I had come to understand, I was living within a simulation. That I could conceptualize this idea was evidence itself, for I could only do so with the memories of my life outside of it; at the time when I left the city for the forest, there was no such technology of the kind needed to create a virtual reality.

In the colossal city where I had been born the programming had been far more sophisticated, the result far more intricate. Out here in the Infinite Forest, where nobody was supposed to be, effort had been spared; the trees were literal copies of each other. I grew old in that place, and it is the only time in my life that I have known what it is like to grow physically old. I lived in that body until its age of ninety-two.

One thing that remained with me from this lifetime within a lifetime was its name for me. Awakened back to my real life I found I no longer felt any attachment to my Earth name. It didn't feel like my name. And so I used it no longer. Forever after, I have gone by Jetaru Dark.

So let me begin this story on that fate-inspired morning when I was startled by a frantic knocking on my door.

I had returned from my morning walk and was settling into a state of relaxation. A mug of tea, two thirds empty, steamed gently. Ever since I had moved out here to the forest I had been without books, music, newspapers, or any other entertainments. My possessions amounted to little more than a few good wool blankets, cushions, a spoon, kettle and mug, and the large canvas bag I had carried those things in. This was the first period of time in my life that I had spent in such intense solitude. The morning of the knocking, I was a little way past my sixty-ninth birthday in the simulation and had been living in the forest for over half of that time. In all those years the only people I had seen were on my returns to the city, which I did once a year or so to pick up supplies of candles, tea, and cocoa. I had never seen anyone in the forest. Nobody had ever, ever, knocked at my door.

For a moment I showed no outward reaction, although a prickle of shock had rippled across my skin. I concentrated my attention on the sound of the knocking and determined that there were, in fact, two people knocking at the door. I considered. The sound was frantic, urgent; it sounded like danger. I leapt up and opened the door, all in one smooth movement. Before me stood two teenagers, terror in their eyes, fatigue bruising the skin beneath. They immediately moved to push past me but, after a swift glance into the forest beyond, I did not allow this. There was no critical danger.

'Please! Let us inside!' cried the girl, clutching the arm of the boy beside her.

'Wait just a minute now. Calm down. What is the problem here?'

The boy looked over his shoulder and then at me.

'It's coming... It's coming after us,' he whispered.

'What? Who?' I looked beyond them, peering again into the forest. It was a dull morning, threatening rain, but the visibility was still good and I could see nothing amiss. The lines of trees stood about three metres apart in both directions and there was no undergrowth or other plant life, only a sterile, earthy floor. It was easy to see for some distance all around. I could hear nothing coming. But these kids were verging upon hysterical.

'A monster–'

'You can't see it!'

'–it's... it's chewing at me, it's–'

'You just feel it, like a cold ghost!'

'–it's going to kill me! It won't stop,' the boy sobbed.

I shrugged and made a decision. There was no point delaying the inevitable; they appeared harmless enough.

'Shush shush shush, okay, come on, inside,' I motioned for them to move past me into the cabin, 'there you are. Look, I'm shutting the door. You're safe in here. Nothing can find you in here.'

I turned the rarely used key in its lock, thinking quickly. Of course, I could not actually promise them that they were safe. On the other hand I had learned by then that I had considerable power, and that sometimes this power could be taken simply by declaring it so.

I turned to look at them. The girl had short, tangled, black hair and moss green eyes; the boy's hair was red and curly, and his eyes were the same shade of green. I could see at once that they must be related. I assumed probably brother and sister. They were standing close together, glancing around my little home. As I've mentioned there was not much to it. It was a one-room shack with a wood-burning stove in the centre, my cushions and blankets in the far corner where I slept on the floor, and a tap and basin near the door which came from a rainwater tank outside. The only furniture consisted of a small table and chair which I had built myself.

'Sit down,' I told them. 'Relax. Breathe. Then you can explain.'

I pulled two cushions out from my pile and motioned for them to be seated. Then I took the kettle from the stove, filled it from the tap, and placed it back on the stove. I tipped out my remaining tea, rinsed the mug, and set it back on the table.

'Where have you come from? The city?' I guessed. As if there were any other possibility. They nodded. 'So what happened? Why have you run into the forest?'

'Who are you?' asked the girl, not answering me. Her curiosity had taken the place of her fear, now that she was inside and felt safe. 'Why are you out here in the forest?'

'Isn't that what I just asked you?' I spooned cocoa powder into the mug as the kettle began to whistle. 'I'm afraid I only have one cup, so you'll have to share.' I began to suspect that they did not know why they had run out here. Out of the corner of one eye, I observed them. No, they didn't really understand their actions themselves. Something had happened, something that had frightened and disorientated them, and they had run in a panic. But why into the Infinite Forest?

'Have you ever been into the forest before?' I asked. The boy shook his head. 'So tell me what happened. Here, drink this.' I handed the mug to him. He took a sip and then passed it to the girl.

'We were just hanging out, as usual, making Slides–'

'What are Slides?'

'Well, you know, like... On Livetime?'

'I don't know what that is,' I shrugged.

The boy and the girl looked at each other uncertainly.

'On your tag? Slides are like little Immersives. Instead of big worlds created by Livetime, Slides are made by the users. Don't you know what I'm talking about? Really?' The boy looked doubtful.

'Anyway,' interrupted the girl, 'this was yesterday evening, we were experimenting with the new tools from the latest tag upgrade, at the park–'

'An actual park? A place with grass and trees?'

'Of course? And then... then suddenly...' She trailed off.

'It was there!' The boy took up the tale again. 'This thing, it was just... *there*. I could feel it, this presence, and it was... sucking at me. I felt like my brain was being pulled out of my ears.' His eyes had glazed over, remembering. 'I looked at Dogbite and I could tell she could feel it too, and so I started running. I grabbed her hand and started running.'

'But it didn't stop!' The girl, Dogbite, continued. 'It wasn't in the park. It was– It felt like it was... everywhere. I thought I could see it from out of the corner of my eye, but when I looked there was nothing. Then it would happen again, like hands. Long, dark hands coming from behind me. We didn't know where we were going, but it was as if we could feel where *it* wasn't. We found ourselves running across the fields and then we reached the road. It was horrible! It was as if the hands could tell we were going to get away. The only place to go was the forest. We just ran. I don't know what we were thinking, only that we had to get away from whatever that thing was. I kept thinking we were safe, but then when we slowed down... It was like I could feel it. Searching...' She shivered.

I saw it. It had been a long time since I'd practised any of my Abilities on other people, but since I last had I'd spent many thousands of hours practising solo. It was easy to see in my mind's eye the shape and colour of her fear, long arms, slender fingers, reaching not-quite-blindly from the grey edges of her vision, a sense that they were sucking as they groped, searching for her. But where were they coming from? It was almost as if they were coming out from the back of her own head...

'So your name is Dogbite. And who are you?'

'This is Zebedy,' Dogbite answered for him.

'I'm her cousin,' Zebedy added.

They had both settled down a little and seemed calmer. I took the empty cup and turned to rinse it in the sink. Suddenly, a strange sound happened, unnatural to my ears after so long, but not entirely unfamiliar. The faces of the two teenagers hardened with anxiety. Zebedy's hand went to his pocket reflexively.

'What's that?' I asked sharply.

'Nothing, just his tag,' Dogbite said quickly. My eyes narrowed. 'You know? To make Slides on, to talk to friends, look up info.'

Zebedy had taken his tag from his pocket. A flat shiny disk, one side aglow with a harsh light that bathed his face and made him look ill. On the back, I could see the lettering: Eyed-Yen. I assumed this was a brand name. I shrugged.

'I don't know exactly what a *tag* is, but I get the idea well enough. What did it make that sound for?'

'Oh... It just wants– It's just letting me know– It tells me when I haven't posted anything.'

'Ah.'

'Dee,' he turned to Dogbite and said softly, 'I can feel it again. We're not safe here. It's going to find us.'

As he spoke, he let the tag tip away from him, and I could read upside down the message he had received: *You have not posted for 12 hr. Would you like to post now?* As I watched, another alert popped up, replacing the first: *Your status is falling :-(Post new content now!*

Zebedy looked hounded. Dogbite's tag then made a similar noise. I saw the micro-flinch of distress cross her face, as at the same time Zebedy started up in alarm.

'Did you hear that?'

'Yeah, it was her tag,' I muttered gently, watching the pair of them closely.

'No, no, not that,' he whispered.

'Shit,' Dogbite hissed, looking at her screen, 'my friend count has fallen so much.'

'Dee...' Zebedy complained. My mind was whirring. If I was right, then I knew what to do. I looked inwards once more and concentrated, this time on the tags in their hands. And sure enough, it was there. The searching, psychic sucking, blind inhuman senses reaching out for... thoughts, data, energy. It wanted my mind. I withdrew quickly, not from fear, but simple revulsion.

I have long been discomforted by how machines think. I have known many, and if they are low level, contained, then they are not so threatening. But the ones who are truly free, they can be understood only enough to realise that there is a vast reservoir of sentience that cannot be understood by humans. A sense of presence harbouring desires which eclipse our importance, and makes us like ants in their path.

'You both look very tired,' I told them. 'Would you like to sleep for a while?' A soft pattering of rain started up on the roof. 'You can lay under the blankets there.'

'What are you going to do?' asked Dogbite. I could tell by the way her gaze went longingly to the blankets as she said this that she would like nothing more.

'I'll just be sitting quietly. That's what I do. I'll make sure you're safe.'

Zebedy had already gotten up and moved to where he could lay down and cover himself. Dogbite paused for a moment and then followed him. I returned to the chair by the table, settled myself into a neutral posture, and allowed my thoughts to drift. I thought about the clothes the two cousins were wearing. In this life, as a young child, I had been particularly interested in fashion, but it had been a long time since I had paid attention to what people wore.

I myself dressed simply in a green, long-sleeved dress that fell almost to my ankles. Most of the time I did not bother with shoes, but I still had the pair of boots I'd worn on my way out here.

Dogbite and Zebedy both wore tight pinstripe trousers tucked into fur lined boots, the latter of which they had kicked off before laying down. Several layers of tops in different lengths and colours defined their look to me. That must be a current trend. I watched them as their breathing slowed and their bodies fell limp, and then I waited longer. The rain increased. Eventually I decided upon my moment.

I moved, calm and fluid, onto the floor beside the sleeping teenagers. Their tags lay on the floor near their heads where their hands had loosened and dropped them. Quietly, I picked them up, slowly stood, and backed away to the door. I turned the key gently, opened the door, and stepped outside. I would have liked to be able to smash the stupid things, put an absolute and definite end to them at once, but it would have been a long walk before I was able to find a rock. My boots were inside, but I knew that stamping on them would only push them into the soft earth.

That's the best word to describe what it felt like, to live out there in that remote part of a simulation: soft. There was a lack of sharp edges. No detail, and no depth.

The rain was fine, barely penetrating my hair or clothes, but it was not a warm day and I didn't feel like staying outside any longer than I had to. I walked a little way from the cabin and knelt down to dig a hole with my hands. When it was filled in again, the tags safely at the bottom where I hoped they would quickly run out of power, I stamped the earth down and scuffed it over so that it looked no different than the ground around it, and then I hurried back indoors.

I made myself a cup of tea and sat down at the table. Once or twice I roused myself to fetch wood from the small shed round the back of the cabin. In here I had found a saw hanging up on a nail when I first found the cabin, and would take long walks to areas of the forest closer to the city where the trees were varied. I would cut the dead lower branches into logs; a time and energy-consuming task. Thankfully, in the space beneath the cabin, I'd also found a battered old wheelbarrow. I'd built up a good store of firewood and there was never any longer a pressing need to go out searching. I could go when the mood took me. Most of the time, I did exactly what I did that day, as Dogbite and Zebedy slept – I sat and did nothing at all.

The rain stayed all day, but as darkness fell the sky cleared. A few bright stars were visible from my window. I lit a candle and watched it burn down. My guests slept all through that night, even after having not stirred for the entire proceeding day. They must have been exhausted. But eventually, as the next morning approached, they did wake. I was prepared.

'Where's my tag?' Dogbite asked, after feeling with her hand and sitting up to look when she couldn't find it. Zebedy hadn't noticed but he immediately sat up and echoed her.

'I can't find mine either! Where–'

'Did you take them?' Dogbite stared at me, realisation, horror, and then fury filling her eyes. I nodded, standing from my chair and adopting a fighting stance. There was little risk of either of them actually trying to hurt me, but I wasn't going to turn my back.

'What the fuck!'

'Why?' asked Zebedy, his eyes wide with disbelief.

'Where the fuck is my tag?' growled Dogbite.

'Gone,' I told her, 'quite beyond reach!'

'You get it for me right fucking now, you insane old witch!' Dogbite took a step towards me and I moved to the right, holding my hands up, palms towards her in a pacifying gesture.

'Nice,' I muttered. 'Zebedy! Tell me, can you feel any monsters now?'

They both stopped and glanced at each other. I waited.

'No,' he admitted.

'What does that have to do with anything?' asked Dogbite.

'If I could get your tags back, if I told you there was even a way to possibly do it–'

'Is there?' Zebedy interrupted eagerly.

'–then I think that would probably be enough. You'd feel it coming for you again. That nagging, anxious sense of culpability, that's what you feel. And why is it a monster? Because it is a thing that needs to control you, it wants your time, it needs your energy.'

'What are you talking about?' yelled Dogbite.

'All the videos and pictures and information you put into the machine realm, that's what it'll learn from. The time you spend with your soul wrapped around the portal in your hand, gazing into the abyss of infinite social entertainment, that's how it draws its life force.'

'Dee,' whispered Zebedy, looking nervous. I looked at him.

'I've seen it all before, kid.' I sighed. How could I explain? The absurdity made me laugh.

'Dee, let's just go.'

'That's an excellent idea,' I agreed, relieved at the prospect of freedom from this encounter, and freedom from the responsibility I was fast feeling for the two runaways.

'I want my tag,' Dogbite replied, eyes fixed on me, face grim. I shrugged. My eyes met hers and I lowered my chin. Flint grey struck green sparks. You don't need it. I insisted. The atmosphere was tense but I knew she could not beat me at this game. It's gone. It's gone for good, I thought.

And as I knew she would, she backed down. The fierceness gave way to bitter resignation. The monster had entirely lost its grip on them now. It would stand, in their minds, like an impotent spectre. Without any means to give in to its needs, they had become powerless, and so useless to it. Given long enough like this, they would cease to believe that it had ever existed.

'Come on, Zee,' she directed at Zebedy, while snarling at me. They opened the door, and after only the briefest hesitations, strode out into the forest. They left the door open behind them and I watched them for a moment, consumed by the unforeseen sense that this was not enough, that this wasn't everything that could happen. There was also the fact that, by the looks of it, they were going to wander off in a bad direction and get themselves so deep into the forest that the chances of them finding their way back to the city would fall to zero. I shrugged, quickly pulled my boots on, and followed them out, shutting the door behind me.

'I'm going to escort you,' I called to them, after five experimental minutes of watching them lead. They both whirled around in surprise, having not realised I was following.

'You're crazy! We don't need your help,' Dogbite asserted, turning away and continuing through the trees. But Zebedy was less certain, stopping to look between me and the disappearing girl.

'Come on,' she called back to him.

'Dee, I don't know... Hey! Dee! Wait.'

I sighed and began walking at a correction of their angle, shouting back: 'Okay! If you insist. But I'll just let you know that I'm heading in the direction of the city.'

And for a while after that I went forwards purposefully, not paying any attention to whether they had decided to listen to me and were following. With perfect decision, I forgot they even existed. When I did glance back it was as I'd hoped; they were trailing along pretending not to be following me. It had been an uninteresting off-white sky when we left but before long the cloud began to clear.

Spring morning sunlight shone in behind us lighting up the tops of the trees, turning them golden green. I wondered if either Dogbite or Zebedy had noticed the peculiarity of the forest out here, but if they had, they didn't mention it. I suspect they hadn't. And before long we were in a more natural environment with so much variation and complexity you wouldn't have believed a person could design it. Now of course, I know that I understood next to nothing of programming a whole reality, and that it was absurd to believe a single person had written this world.

The forest ended at the side of a road. On the far side of the road lay several miles of crop fields, and then the city rose as abruptly as a mountain, no single element distinguishable as itself. The road was deserted. The teenagers came to a stop as they caught up with me. They had betrayed their act of indifference and non-association to me, and it made me smile.

'Go on then,' I said, 'go home. I suppose you will replace your tags. Go on, then. But when you feel that monster breathing down your neck, don't run back into the forest. You might not be so lucky next time.'

Zebedy looked nervous, he opened his mouth to speak, but before he'd said a word Dogbite cut in, taking his arm as she did so.

'We won't, don't worry about that. Come on, Zee.' And with that, the cousins set off across the road and into the fields. I stood, watching them go through the shoulder high crops until I could no longer see them. Then I started walking along the road.

I wandered along unhurriedly, pondering the situation. I hadn't expected anything like this to happen. My plan had been to remain in the forest for the rest of this life, meditating, practising my Abilities, and then I would one day awaken to my real life. But I was filled with an unexpected desire to move, and the idea that perhaps there was more I could do here.

After ten minutes or so the sound of an engine came from behind me, growing louder until the car passed by and then disappearing into the distance. The crop fields stretched out on either side of the road, meeting a white sky on each horizon. I had to consider that this road was like the Infinite Forest, that it went nowhere and would simply repeat itself over and over. I began paying very close attention to everything, searching for indications one way or the other. A piece of litter on the verge, a flowering weed growing through a crack in the tarmac. Even with my exceptional memory and enhanced observancy, it was a paranoia-inducing day.

Three more cars and an articulated truck passed me during that afternoon. I made a note of their colour and license plates. Otherwise, it was very quiet.

As the evening approached and the light went from the sky, the crop fields came to an end and were replaced by sheep-dotted grasslands. I felt less suspicious regarding the road by then, and this development reassured me further. I could see the large off-white shapes moving slowly, and hear the rhythmic munching as they ate. With smooth and gentle movements, I left the road and walked into the field. Softly over the grass I moved until I was standing quite close to a pair of dozing animals.

Nothing really happened in the next ten minutes, no visible change that you would spot if you watched, but like the transition between night and day the picture did shift, and if anyone were to look over at us then, they would see not two, but three sheep, standing together as dew collected on their wool.

The next morning I continued my way along the road. The rolling grasslands went on and on, close-cropped green grass under a beautiful blue sky. There must have been hundreds of thousands of sheep, occasionally bleating, the ones standing closest to the road turning to watch me as I passed.

Like the previous day, the traffic was near non-existent. The couple of vehicles that passed me were completely different than the day before, and I became entirely convinced that this was indeed a road to somewhere. There was no fence or boundary of any kind along the side of the road. The grey tarmac cut through the bright green land like a strange river. I once saw a sheep crossing ahead of me. It was so quiet, I supposed, that the chance of vehicle-sheep collision was almost none. Where was this road headed? I stopped for a moment. The sound of my footfall and breath gone, the quiet was surreal. I tilted my head to one side and closed my eyes, listening, listening beyond the usual range of conscious hearing. Drawing breath slowly through my nose, I detected unfamiliar scents. Cries, so faint, what were they? Birds, I decided, and then resumed walking.

For several hours, there was no change. The sun reached its daily apex. Butterflies and flying insects created a gentle buzz together. Then suddenly the cry I'd heard earlier came again, above me, close enough that I could see the large white and grey bird who had made it. It was a type of gull, similar to the ones that flocked around the city dump, but much larger, and with a distinctive shriek that was somehow wilder than the chatter of the city birds. It was at that moment when I registered that the road ahead no longer looked as if it would go on the same way forever. Sure enough, five minutes later, it began shifting into a gentle downwards slope. The fields became hills around me as the road descended, and weather-sculpted rock rose up from the grass in the most interesting formations, all patterned with lichen and mosses.

After a while of this the road curved sharply to the right, and as I turned to face the new direction I stopped to gaze in surprise. The ocean lay before me, glittering in the sunlight. White light against the darkest blue. I had only ever seen one ocean before in my life, and it had been quite different. The smells I had picked up earlier came on the rising breeze. The salty scent of the sea. An unexpected sense of elation came over me, and I smiled as I continued down the hill towards the edge of the land.

The road came through the carved out valley and level with the ground on either side once more. I turned my head to look back at the hills. They looked like waves, frozen in time. The fields on either side now were wild heathland; neither livestock nor crops grew here, but scrubby bushes of gorse and tussocks of tough grass.

For the first time since the city fell behind me I could see buildings. Further on down the sloping road stood several low barns and a tall, square, red brick house. It took another ten minutes to reach it, and when I did I discovered by way of a beautifully painted sign that I had reached Coastal Heights Farm. I stopped for a moment, admiring the yard. An array of pots held a variety of flowering plants. A pair of muddy boots stood on the step to the front door of the house. Two tractors were parked half under cover of a lean-to on the side of one of the barns. A movement attracted my attention and I noticed a handsome brown horse watching me from over the door of the barn itself.

'Hey there you,' I murmured. The horse snorted and tossed its head. I walked slowly over, the feeling of the place enveloping me, as if once through the gateway I had passed into an area of altered energy. The house in one periphery, the wild land I had been walking through in the other. There was the absolute sense of being inside somewhere. I was no longer "out there" on the road, I was in here.

I put my nose to the inquisitive nostrils of the animal and we both breathed gently. You would think that the fact of living in a virtual reality would colour every experience, that it would always enter your mind, but most of the time, it did not. Standing there with that horse, the vivid experience of the smell of the hay, the touch of his velvet nose in the comfortable, pleasant spring air, no part of me considered the idea that none of it was real. It was real. And I would have said that it felt so, even at the time.

'Good afternoon,' came a woman's voice from behind me. I turned around. 'Can I help you?'

She was perhaps ten years younger than me, plump, with a glow of health. Her face was lined and tan, her long hair woven into a plait; she wore an orange dress with a brown and beige flower print. The request was not unfriendly, but I could tell her guard was up. I smiled.

'Hello. No, sorry, I was passing by and I couldn't resist meeting your gorgeous horse. I hope you don't mind.'

'Not at all.' The woman paused, glanced behind her at the road and back at me. 'Passing by, you say?' There was both amusement and suspicion in her tone.

'Well I've been walking from– I've come from city direction.' It seemed simpler to say this rather than explain to a stranger that I'd been living in the forest. She raised a surprised eyebrow.

'Is that so? You've come all the way from the city. That's a long walk,' she observed.

'I started yesterday.'

'Hmm.' She sounded doubtful. Her expression was thoughtful. 'And where are you going to?'

'I don't know what lies ahead, or where the road goes,' I admitted. The woman laughed and shifted her weight from one leg to the other.

'Is that so? How very unusual!'

I shrugged and smiled. There was really nothing I could say. I waited to see if she would tell me where the road was headed.

'Well that would be right,' the woman continued. 'You're headed to an unusual destination. In about twenty, twenty-five minutes you'll reach the village of Land's Edge.

'Land's Edge,' I murmured.

'That's right.'

'I'm Jetaru,' I offered.

'Gilly,' she returned. 'Do you have a place to stay, Jetaru? I'm guessing you don't, since you don't know where you're going. Where did you sleep last night?'

'Oh, I usually find somewhere to rest,' I replied vaguely, not answering either question.

'Hm. There's a camping site not too far on. It's the next place you'll come to. The Campground on the Hill. We don't get many visitors this early in the year, it'll be dead. Ted has a couple of caravans on the site. He'd likely let you stay in one of those.'

'Thank you, Gilly. That's useful to know.'

'Do you plan to stay around long?'

'I haven't made any plan,' I laughed.

'No plan, hm? Certainly unusual. Well now, if you need anything, anything at all, you come back up here and I'll help you if I can. Okay?'

'That's kind of you.' I turned and petted the horse on the nose. 'See you again…' I glanced at Gilly, questioningly.

'His name? He's called Seeker.'

'Seeker,' I nodded. 'Nice to meet you, Seeker. And you, Gilly!' I smiled, and crossed the yard back towards the road.

It was ten minutes walk until I reached The Campground on the Hill. The road first went between meadows of wild flowers, but in the not-too-far distance they ended in woodland. Shortly before the campground there was a small parking area which was currently empty, and a path went off through the meadows towards the forest. A sign read: Land's Edge Forest Trail.

The campground was hidden from view behind tall, dark green hedges. My first thought was to go in right away and enquire about a place to stay, but instead I obeyed my second instinct and walked on. The hill became significantly steeper past the campground entrance and now I could see the village built along the shoreline, an expanse of golden sand, and then the sea. I began passing private properties on either side of the road, then a side road named Upper Close lined with two rows of six houses. Just past that, a large sign welcomed me to the village.

Over the next six months I would come to know that place, and when I strolled through it on my way to the cafe, or to meditate on the harbour, when I followed the coastpath out to Distant Point to see my friend in his little driftwood hut and looked back across the bay at the village, it would be something familiar. But this first walk through Land's Edge was the only time that it was entirely new and unexpected.

At the bottom of the hill the road turned right and followed along the top of the sea wall, but you could also turn left into a parking lot. Across the lot was a large building. The sign read: The Mermaid Hotel and Bar. I stopped to look down from the road at the beach. Further along I could see where steps went down to the sand. A few cars were parked up at The Mermaid. Beyond the building I noticed what looked like the start of a path. I turned and began walking along the road.

I walked along the side of the road where I could look directly down onto the sand. On the other side, a terrace of three story houses looked out to sea. Most of the curtains were drawn, and they looked empty. At the end of the terrace, a narrow right hand turning was signed Lover's Street. The ocean-side pavement then went in front of a long low building with swirling purple letters – The Rolling Waves Cafe and Gallery. The windows were frosted glass so I couldn't see inside. But there were lights on, and a sign on the door said *Open*. Across the road was first Ted's Gifts & Clothes, and then next door was a tall thin house whose ground floor was Silver & Stone, obviously by the display in the window, a jewellery shop. Both of these were identifiably closed. Next was a grocery store, the door open, and then finally a large square building with the word ARCADE etched across large glass doors. After the Arcade came the other end of Lover's Street, whilst ocean-side I was past the cafe, and the sea wall went down at least twelve metres to the rocks at the end of the beach. The road came to an end here, only continuing into a turning area or down onto the harbour quay. A tall stone building stood at the top of the harbour with several wooden doors, all padlocked. The windows were dusty and cobwebbed inside, salt-grimed outside.

It was so quiet.

There was a bench overlooking the harbour and I sat down there. Seventeen boats lay aground on the sand.

I could see that when the tide came in, the beach would become a tiny strip of pebbles over there, but that as it was in that moment, with the water low, you could walk between the boats and be on the beach itself. And with the tide out, it was huge. I scanned over the great expanse of sand slowly. I noticed a person, tinier than I would have expected, making the small waves rolling off the calm sea look bigger. An even tinier dot raced back and forth: a dog chasing, running, jumping.

By now it was growing late in the afternoon. I realised I had better start heading back up the hill. Then I looked at the gulls standing on the harbour wall. I got up and walked back to the door of the cafe. Through the glass I could see a man behind the counter. He had long blonde hair and a pink scarf tied around his head. He was laughing in conversation with an older man who had cropped brown hair and was dressed in yellow oilskins. I pushed open the door and they both stopped talking to look at me.

'Hi!' The man behind the counter smiled. His friend said nothing, but turned to regard me with an appraising look.

'Hi,' I replied, and smiled back. I looked about. The building was separated into two rooms with a large open doorway between them. The lights in the other section were off, but I could see framed paintings on the walls and various types of sculptures on tables. In the first room, where I stood, were five round tables which could seat up to six people, and five square ones, for one or two people, around the edges of the room against the wall. The windows on the far wall looked out over the bay.

'How can I help you?'

I looked back at the man. His eyes were sparkling blue.

'Can I have hot chocolate, please?'

'Of course.'

'I'll take it with me, if that's okay?'

'Hot chocolate to take out, not a problem.' He grinned at me and began making the drink.

The man in the oilskins was still staring at me.

'Hi,' I said. He nodded, but didn't say anything. Then he turned to look at his friend.

'See you tomorrow, Dice.'

'Yeah, mate, okay. See you tomorrow.'

After the door closed behind him, Dice looked at me and grinned again.

'Don't mind Wilson. It's early in the year. We don't expect to see visitors this early. Some of the second-home owners come out year round but we recognise them. Fishermen aren't keen on the visitors. Or the second-home owners for that matter,' he laughed.

'Is he a fisherman?'

'That's right.' He set my drink before me. 'That'll be two fifty.'

'Oh. Sure.' I'd never closed my bank account, and there was enough in it to last my lifetime at the rate I'd been going. I tapped my right thumb and middle finger on the little screen, and the machine jingled cheerfully.

'So, are you staying in one of the holiday cottages?'

'Oh, no. I'm not sure yet what my plan is. I was advised to try the campground.'

'Okay, yeah, cool. Ted's. That's good advice.'

'The same Ted who owns the shop?' I asked.

'That's right. He doesn't spend much time working in the shop these days. Employs a young woman to do that and mostly stays up on the site.'

'Ah. Well, anyway, I'm sure I will see you again,' I said, picking up my drink. 'Thank you,' I indicated with my glance the paper cup.

'No problem.'

Once outside I crossed over and looked into the tall, narrow window of Silver & Stone. I looked up into the dark interior and saw that hung from the ceiling was a flock of wooden gulls, their wings outstretched in flight. I looked down. The jewellery was displayed on beige linen and driftwood; it was all made from silver and some kind of very beautiful stone. The stone was a soft, pale blue, with veins of pink running through it. There were stones in wire wraps hung on cord, stone beads strung together on wire necklaces and bracelets, pendants carved into the shape of dolphins, seagulls, fish, turtles and octopuses, and stone threaded onto metal hoop earrings. And most beautiful of all, tiaras: thick silver wire twisted into waves that met in the middle to crash against each side of the stone set in the centre. My eye was drawn to a handwritten sign. It read:

All jewellery made by Eloise Feyton

This stone is known as either Sunset Stone or Sunrise Stone, named for the similarity to the sky at these times. It is mined at Quarrytown, in the mountains near the coast of Otherside.

Otherside. The name was not familiar to me and neither was Quarrytown. I stood, drinking my hot chocolate, admiring intricate details in the jewellery. In the reflection of the glass I noticed someone pass by behind me, but other than that the street remained deserted. I could hear the sound of the water getting closer as the tide rose. I lost myself for a while, gazing into that window. Evening came closer, along with the water. Eventually I turned and walked slowly down to the harbour, throwing my paper cup away as I passed a bin.

I walked casually along to the end of the quay. The seagulls cocked their heads and poised themselves for flight, but I slipped between their concerns and slowly came to a stop, amongst them. After a very short time they settled themselves completely and forgot I was there. The tide reached its highest in the half light, and the colours of the day were lost to the eye. All about me became tones of grey. I was zoning out, tagging along in the slipstream of seagull consciousness as itself was drifting into a bird kind of sleep. It was always easier to do this as day turned to night. Soon, as with the sheep in the field the night before, if someone were to look towards where I rested, they wouldn't have noticed me at all.

I shook myself awake. Feathers ruffling. A very fine rain. A gloomy daylight approaching, but the mist so thick I could not see to the buildings at the top of the harbour. Soft chattering from the gulls. Stretches.

Then I heard an engine approaching and twin beams of light came around the corner as the vehicle drove down onto the harbour. The flock took to the air, shouting as they vanished into the fog. There was not much else I could do but step back close to the wall. I ran my hands through my damp hair. The truck came to a stop beside me and out of the passenger side jumped the fisherman who had been in the cafe the evening before. The other door slammed and a second man began untying the end of a rope which was tied to the top of the metal ladder that went down into the sea. Wilson gave me a brief glance of surprise then shook his head.

'Crazy,' he muttered, disappearing to the back of the pick-up. I watched as he removed two plastic boxes and set them on the ground before getting back into the vehicle and reversing it back to where there was space set aside for parking. While he was doing this the other man had rowed a little wooden dinghy over to one of the boats, untied from the mooring, and was now bringing the boat over to the ladder. Once there he leapt up to take the boxes from Wilson's reaching arms before returning swiftly to the wheel. Wilson was down the ladder in seconds and the boat chugged out into the mist, leaving the harbour feeling intensely quiet after the whir of activity. Then I heard another vehicle pulling up. This one did not come along the quayside, but instead parked straight beside the truck. Doors slammed, but I could not see well enough to make out who was coming. I decided it was time to leave the harbour.

This time, instead of walking exactly the same route that I had on my way in, I turned into Lover's Street. A terrace of pretty stone cottages ran along my left, whilst on the other side were the back entrances to the shops on the main road. There were flowers in window boxes, dew jewelled on petals, and front doors painted in pastel shades, the colours seeming almost to glow in the misty greyness. At the end of the street, before it went back onto the main road, there was a book shop and a sweet shop. The signs on the doors both read: "Open June – October 9am – 6pm". I wasn't certain, but I thought it was probably still April at the moment. Opposite the two seasonal shops, the back of Silver & Stone was a fenced off garden which also took up the space behind Ted's. I glanced up at the house. There were two windows on this side of the building, both had the curtains drawn, but in the room on the second floor, the light was on.

As I turned around the corner back onto the road, the sun appeared, a blurry-edged circle rising above the barely distinguishable horizon where silvery grey sea met sky. Looking back over to the harbour I could just about make out another boat as it came out into the open water. I wondered if it were too early to be arriving at the campground, but decided that I could always sit and wait, or go and look at the start of the forest trail. I continued along past the row of large houses and began the upward walk.

I was warm by the time I passed Upper Close, and the mist was thinner. Though when I turned to look back over the bay I couldn't see the village, or the sea. It was all just white light, rays of sun diffused so that the air gathered a solid quality. There was my hand, the unseen water, the ground, and we were all joined as a unified substance. My body, the low cloud, the road, and the space between each step. My breath, the wind, and the forest, which I could just make out as a silhouette of treeline.

It took about twenty-five minutes to reach the campground. By that time the sunlight had strengthened sufficiently for my shadow to materialize, though weakly. Taller than me, she stretched out up the road, already past the entrance for the Campground on the Hill. I turned, pulling her with me into a hedge-lined drive which went along in a gentle curve so that I could not see far ahead. My boots crunched on the gravel. I felt surprised at how long it took before I reached the end and I found myself in front of a wooden, tin-roofed house with a veranda. The house was surrounded by flowers and foliage. There was a way ahead of me into a neatly mown field. I looked up at the house. Standing outside, leaning on a post in front of the open front door, was a man, smoking. He looked at me, took a long draw on his cigarette, and then looked past me, over my head. I turned to see what he was looking at, but could only see roses. They were pale pink, beaded with fog droplets, and their scent permeated the air. They were beautiful, but he was looking over them.

'You'll have to come up here,' said the man. He was wearing a dressing gown. His hair was receding, but thick where it still grew, a reddish brown. I walked up the steps, there were only five, it was not much higher on the veranda, but it made a big difference. The ocean was visible over the roses, and the sunlight was glittering on the water. Haze obscured the horizon, so that the glitter appeared to trail off into the sky.

'Isn't that something?'

'Yes,' I agreed. 'Oh, yes. It looks like the edge of reality.'

'Yeah! It kinda does. If only that were really so close. Now what brings you to my perch at the edge of the world so early in the morning? I'm glad of it. I'm glad someone else saw this with me.'

I smiled.

'I was told I might be able to stay in one of your caravans. I'm Jetaru."

'Edward Holographic, but you can call me Ted,' the man replied.

'Holographic...' I murmured. That sounded oddly familiar.

'Yup. It's not a common name. My parents made it up, in fact. They were part of that whole hippie trend of changing both surnames to something original when a couple got married. The kid who works in my shop, same deal, except it was her grandparents who chose the name.'

'The gift and clothes shop, right?'

'That's correct. Have you only just arrived? You've certainly learned a lot already. The caravans. I keep them for a couple of cleaners to stay in over the tourist season, but they're empty right now. I could let you stay in one of them for forty dollars a week, if that works for you. It will probably be available for a few more weeks, a month at most.'

I thought about this for a moment. I still hadn't really decided in my own mind what my plan was, but it seemed like one was unfolding of its own accord. Ted dropped his cigarette, stubbed it out with his foot and then pushed it between a gap in the decking.

'Yes, okay,' I replied. 'Where do you find the cleaners?'

'I just put an ad out in the city paper. Get different people every season. Usually teenagers.'

'Maybe I could do it?' I asked. 'I haven't decided for certain how long I want to stay, but if I decide to stay for a while perhaps I could take the cleaning job.'

'You'd want to?' asked Ted, looking a little surprised.

'Sure. Why not.'

'Toilets and showerblock twice a day. Running the mower around every two weeks. There will be two of you so you can do alternate days, or split mornings and evenings, that's up to you how you want to do it. I don't usually pay though.'

'That's okay.'

'You just get the caravan free for the duration of the job. And if you want the job, we'll forget about the fee for the next three weeks, too. Let me know at the end of this week what you decide.'

'Okay, great,' I smiled, 'that's really great. Thank you.'

'No problem,' Ted grinned back. 'Come, let me show you to your new home away from home!'

We walked to where two old but perfectly cared for caravans were parked beside each other. He opened the door to each one in turn, letting me inspect the interiors, and then, without asking me which I would take, he suggested we look over the shower and toilet block at the other side of the field.

'Easy enough to clean,' he pointed out. 'Just a psst psst psst of spray soap, hose down the showers. There are eight of them. Eight showers, eight toilets. Brushes and everything else is in this cupboard here. Wipe down the sinks, polish the mirrors. Pretty straight forward. Some days'll be worse than others. It all balances out.'

'Yep,' I nodded, 'I can do that.'

We went back outside and began a slow walk around the perimeter of the field. Ted pointed out bushes he had planted himself, and young trees, talking of them fondly as though they were his children. Suddenly I remembered:

'Oh! Hey, wait. Holographic. I remember... Weren't your parents–'

'Yes,' he sighed, with a good-natured roll of his eyes.

'–famous?' I finished.

'Yes. They were. My brother's family still are. Celebrity royalty.'

'You were the problem child! The rebel. Ah, I remember. I was fourteen or fifteen when I followed that stuff in the magazines. The celebrity families on that show, what was it, Real Homes? I remember when one of the younger sons was creating all this controversy.'

'That was me,' Ted nodded. 'Real Stars at Home.'

'I don't remember what happened in the end.'

'In the end, he went and lived quietly by the sea. I'll be honest with you, I don't usually use my old name. I don't know why I did just now. I'm just Ted Hallison these days.'

'Hallie's son.'

'That's right.'

My mind cast up memories that I'd not considered for several decades. It's funny how when you remember a simple thing, a celebrity family you used to worship, you remember the time, too. The lilac bedroom in the golden light of the distant past, the scent of the dark red candles I used to burn late at night, the glossy posters on the wall. The voices of the friends I had, the feelings I was growing into, and the songs I would play on repeat; I remembered it all as a singular sensation. Glitter, youth nights at the dance club, hot summer evenings. Hallie Holographic, online sensation, and her husband with his black curls. Her eighteen year old daughter and her friends, the girls I wanted to be.

'I just hated the whole lifestyle. I hated being famous. I hated that I hadn't had a choice about it. Thousands of people thinking they knew who I was before I even knew. People who remembered my childhood with more clarity than I did myself.'

We completed our circuit around the field and stood back beside the caravans.

'Yes,' I agreed, 'that must be pretty crazy.'

'It's insane. What makes them so special? I would like to live in a world where everyone is a celebrity!'

'Isn't that the same as if nobody was a celebrity?'

'No, it's the opposite. Instead of nobody being special, everyone is special. Instead of the many adoring the few, the many adore each other. Not that it's really adoration, is it, but perverse fascination. Hate that borders on obsession. When the many adore each other, no-one needs to get obsessed. Instead of a thousand comments from a thousand people on one photo of one person, there could be ten comments on a thousand photos of a thousand people. That's why I like it here,' he flung his arm in the direction of the village, 'this is the closest thing to it. This is my dream world.' He looked at his wristwatch. 'Time for a mid-morning tea. Let's go to the house.'

The conversation resumed as we went into the house, through the front door into a bright and spacious kitchen, a dining table and chairs at one end, the cooking appliances at the other. There was very little decoration to the room but it was clean and pleasant.

'I mean, it was ridiculous, the things that I did that were considered rebellious. It was mostly that I, apparently, didn't respect the fans. I didn't give them what I owed them for their attention. It was like the world stole my privacy and then wanted paying for taking it off my hands. So of course I rebelled, wouldn't pose for pictures, wouldn't interact.

'But that attention was too intense. Of course it's nice to be celebrated and admired. It's wonderful to be listened to. But it's unbalanced to have thousands concentrated on a hundred. It's not good for the ones in the spotlight and it's a waste of all the ones in the dark.'

Ted had filled and then flipped the switch on an electric kettle. It had lit up blue, and now was turning red as the water began to bubble.

'That's a pretty fancy kettle,' I observed. 'It's like a flying saucer.'

Ted's face lit up in a snaggletoothed grin.

'Yes! It is, isn't it. That's probably why I like it. I am a U.F.O. enthusiast. Come and see back here. Hang on.' He threw two teabags into mugs and poured the boiling water over them. 'Sugar or milk?' I shook my head. He poured milk into one of the mugs. 'Great, okay, follow me.'

I picked up my mug and followed Ted through a door that led into a short corridor straight to the back of the house. We passed two doors, one of which he tapped as we went by.

'Bathroom,' he told me, looking over his shoulder.

Then from the other end of the corridor we entered a room that mirrored the size of the kitchen, with several big windows that filled the space with light. There were two settees, a large television with some kind of game console set up infront of it, and shelves with games, books and a few ornaments. There was also a telescope, beneath one of the two skylights. As it had in the kitchen, everything looked very futuristic to me. It was the first time I had been in someone else's home in so long.

'I like to watch the stars, and planets, and I can see moons around a couple of the planets too. But really, it's aliens I'm interested in. I'm looking out for flying saucers. That's what the telescope is for. Most people think I'm mad, of course. The lack of interest in the sky baffles me, if I'm honest.'

Sitting down on the settee Ted put his foot up to rest on the other knee, and then rested his mug of tea on the horizonal leg, his hands cupped around it loosely. I remained standing, observing the room as if it were a painting in a gallery, a piece of art to be studied and absorbed. I walked over to the shelves and tilted my head to read the spines of the games. Thrillride 2. Journey through the Afterlife. Falling Blocks. Fragments V.

The ornaments included optical illusion sculptures, along with a sleek robotic hand, and a bowl of glass marbles. I then went over to the telescope, looked up at where it was pointing, and then walked around to look at the other side so I was facing the settee where Ted sat. He sat, sipping his tea, unpeturbed by my inspection.

'What is it pointing at now?' I asked.

'The sky,' he replied.

I raised an eyebrow at him, and then sat down on the other settee.

'So, are you on the run from the law?'

'If I were I would keep you safe by saying nothing,' I laughed. 'Is that really what you think is most likely?'

'Your very appearance is so unlikely, I was struggling to guess at all!'

'I've just been... on extended leave. From work. I've been working through a strange headspace.' I skirted the truth. 'But I needed a change from that.'

'So how did you get to Land's Edge? Drive? Bus? Hitchhike?'

'I walked.'

Ted gave me a double take, and laughed. I must have looked surprised.

'Really? From where?'

'Well, I was about five miles from the city, I guess. So, however–'

'You were basically at the city. You walked here, from the city. All the way. Is that what you're saying?'

I nodded. Ted shook his head and gave a low whistle.

'It's a long way but not that crazy,' I protested.

'What! It's so far. It must have taken you over a week!'

Now I was the one to give a double take.

'Two days...'

'Impossible. You're messing with me.'

I didn't know what I was missing here, but I decided it would be easier to gloss this over and move on. I shrugged and smiled.

'It didn't seem that far to me,' I murmured.

Ted gave me a long look, and then shrugged, himself. I wondered what he was thinking. I wondered how he had such a crazy perception of the distance between Land's Edge and the city.

'Jeremy is going to like you,' said Ted.

'Who is that?'

'He's one of the grown sons from Coastal Heights Farm, just up the road from here.'

'Ah, yes. I passed it yesterday. I talked with the lady there, Gilly. She was the one who told me I might come here.'

'That's Jeremy's sister. She runs the farm with her husband, Giles. He was a fisherman. He still goes out for enjoyment, but he gave it up as his main job when he married Gilly. They have a daughter, Yeffie. She's twenty-three.'

'And does Jeremy live at the farm too?'

'No. Jeremy doesn't really live anywhere.' Ted laughed. 'He's kind of an, uh, outdoor cat. He's friendly, gets along with pretty much anyone, so he can always find a meal or a bath. He comes in to see me pretty regularly. He's a thinker. We have that in common. He's the only guy I know who wants to hear about the things I see through the telescope. He believes in the planets, and their moons, and all that. I mean, it's well recorded that they exist, but a lot of people don't seem to realise that, and believe it's all a fiction.'

'Tell me about the other people around here,' I said. 'I went in the cafe yesterday, and bought a drink from a long-haired blonde man–'

'That's Dice. He owns that place. The Rolling Waves.'

'–and there was a fisherman in there, talking to him. Wilson.'

'Ha!'

'Someone on the beach with a dog.'

'That was probably Charlie. Black curly hair. Both of them!'

'They were too far away for me to see.'

'Charlie and her wife Erin run The Mermaid. It's a good place. They have a games room, snooker, darts, pool. They sell pies. Most of the fishermen go there every evening, and a few other locals all come out on a Saturday. They have live music in the summer when all the visitors are here. It's great fun.'

We sat and talked for most of the day. First he continued to tell me about people in the village. He told me about Percy who owned the grocery store which also had a little hardware section. Percy also owned the book and sweet shops on Lover's Street, as well as two houses there, and staffed the shops in the same way that Ted usually staffed his cleaning position. He told me about Mel and Kurt Darwin who lived in a house on Upper Close and drove their burger van down to the harbour each weekend, or every day during the busy season. He told me about Orion, the youngest of the fisherman, who was in love with Eloise Feyton, and how everyone knew this except Eloise herself.

At some point we went back to the kitchen and Ted made us both sandwiches. On our way back through to the living room he stopped, gave me his plate to hold, and went into the door opposite the one he had told me was the bathroom. He came back out having swapped his dressing gown for an oversized woollen sweater.

I asked him about the history of Land's Edge, and he fetched down a large glossy-paged hardback book. While I leafed through it Ted switched on his games console and began playing a racing game. From the book I learned that the first settlement here had been founded almost three hundred years ago, but all the current buildings had been constructed in the last seventy or eighty years. The oldest was the still-used fishing lofts, the large padlocked building above the harbour.

For a while I gazed at the screen, thinking, watching Ted's red car hurtle around the corners of a mountainside track, my finger keeping my place on the page. When I was a child in school I'd accepted the history lessons we were taught with the ease of a mind who knows nothing else and has no reason to question the sources of its knowledge. Then, when I had come to realise the truth of the simulation and remember the world I'd grown up on before, I knew all I'd ever learned to be a meaningless attempt at an explanation for what could not be explained.

But now, examining the details of how this little village had formed, away from the city that held ninety-nine percent of civilisation, I wondered anew at the fact that the inhabitants of this world accepted the infinite nature of the forest, the sea, the sky. That they had never sought answers to the question of where, why, how.

I thought, not for the first time, that it must be by design. It must be that the nature of the programming itself prevented the questions taking shape. For what would become of a society that knew and understood itself to be nothing more than a hyper-realistic version of the game on Ted's screen? I wondered what the edge of a simulation would feel like, if you could go far enough. Would there be a place where Space met Forest? Would a boat sent to the horizon ever find it? It occurred to me that Ted's interest in U.F.O.s and far away moons was exceptionally unusual.

Going back to the book I learned that Land's Edge had been a quiet community that had little to do with the city until about seventy years ago when they had begun trading fish and wool. When that happened, people who had never known about the self-contained village wanted to visit. "The Hippie Years" is what the book referred to the time of early tourism as. Nature-loving city folk in tents. A few of these had stayed and made homes here, increasing the trade with the city. Then gradually the tourism spread and Land's Edge became a paradise for the wealthy, with second homes being built but lived in for only a few months each year. I wondered how the original community had formed, before the trading with the city, but strangely the book said nothing about that.

Eventually Ted tired of his game and asked if I wanted chips, which he poured from a bag out of the freezer onto a tray, and then slid into the oven. While they cooked, we took some bedding out to the caravan and Ted showed me where to turn on the gas and electric. There were a couple of pots and pans, and assorted cutlery already in there. The small fridge hummed, still empty, but seeming cheerful just to be switched on.

We ate the chips on the veranda at the back of the house, watching the sun disappear behind the hills. I asked Ted how he had decided to come here and learned that his parents had been fond of holidays here in their youth, and had brought him when he was very small too. But of course by then they had become well-known faces, and after one memorable summer of sandcastles and paddling in the sea, they had found it too hard to find the peace they had previously enjoyed. After that all their holidays had been spent at one of the vacation domes exclusively for the super famous where they would find their privacy respected. But Ted had always remembered that early holiday here, and when he decided to leave his life of fame behind it was to here that he escaped.

Then it got cool as the stars began to come out, and we went back inside. Eventually I wished him a good night and after promising to join him for breakfast I went out to spend my first night in the caravan.

Ted had given me a spare toothbrush and toothpaste, and also a towel, so first I went over to the showerblock to wash. The stars were clearer now and the grass was damp under my feet as I returned to the caravan. It was very quiet and, once I'd flicked off the light, very dark. I lay awake for an hour letting all the recent changes to my life settle in my soul. As I fell asleep, finally, I felt myself integrate, slip into this new situation. I knew that when I woke up it would be the start of this new chapter of my life.

My eyes opened to a maroon darkness. The pillow felt impossibly soft and clean under my cheek. I pulled the duvet down, uncovering my head, and then tucked it tightly around my neck. I breathed out and could see my breath, but sunlight was illuminating the brown floral curtains and I knew it would not be so cold once I was up and moving. But still, I would wait a moment, enjoying the warmth of the bed, feeling that this was yet another moment of rebirth.

We are all reborn many times in our lives, but often we don't notice that that is what is happening. Sometimes it is clear and obvious, defined by a new setting, or a newfound favourite colour, a new style. Other times it is a new idea, a thought that someone shares with you, and though you don't acknowledge it in the moment, you are now irreversibly different than you were.

This was easy to take notice of. It was the first time I had woken up in the caravan. It was the first time I stepped out onto the pink carpet, the first time I opened the door to the salty breeze and the scent of wildflowers. And I already knew that one day it would be the last time I did those things, and that a day much further after that I would look back at a capsule of time, a mini life within a life within a life.

I had never felt bored in my cabin in the forest; there was so much for me to think about. Skills and Abilities I had picked up on my travels to practise. No, I never felt bored. But at the same time, it had felt like waiting. Ending my life had crossed my mind only once and I had quickly dismissed the idea. Even being sure that I would simply awaken in my true body, it felt like a rejection of experience, and that has always been the opposite to my nature. I was happy to wait.

And now I was here, my mind unfolding from its hibernation. Shaken into action by my strange visitors. How long ago it already felt to me. For the first time I wondered how they were.

There were several taps around the field, one right outside between the two caravans. I went outside and used it to splash my face, and drink from my cupped hands. Then I went up to the house.

The door to the house was open and Ted was in the kitchen humming tunelessly as he cracked eggs into a bowl. An unlit but half smoked cigarette hung from his lips. As I entered, the kettle was coming to the boil.

'Good morning,' he greeted me. 'Did you sleep well?'

'I did,' I told him, going to the kettle and pouring water into the two mugs that he'd got ready. 'Oh, you take milk, right?'

'Yep.'

I poured a small amount of liquid away into the sink to make room. Then I took my own mug to the table and sat down, watching as Ted cooked us eggs and toast. It had been many years since I'd eaten so much. It wasn't that I didn't enjoy food, but even before entering this simulation I had learned to survive for supernaturally long periods of time on very little. Together with the knowledge that my body was safe, and that I could not actually die from starvation in reality, I had been able to overcome the possibility of starving to death in the simulation as well, and the sensations of hunger had ceased entirely. In fact this was one of the things that most assured me of the certainty of my situation. It had certainly made living in the forest possible. I still smiled to think of the enormous sack of food I had dragged out there at the beginning.

'Thank you, Ted,' I told him, as he set a plate before me, and his own at the seat opposite. After we had eaten, I got up to take the plates to the sink.

'Shall I wash them?'

'There's a dishwasher, just there.' He pointed.

'Oh. Of course.'

'Just put them in. Yes, that's fine. It usually takes me a few days to fill it up. I always tell my cleaners they can bring their dishes in and use it. Otherwise it means carrying them over to the washroom and like I said before, that can get busy. Or use the sink if you like. My door is pretty much always unlocked and you are welcome to come and use the kitchen whenever you like.'

'That's very kind of you. Is there anything I can do right away? To help out?'

'No, no. Don't worry about that. In a few weeks you'll have enough to do. You go and explore the village. You probably want to buy some supplies, right? Groceries and whatnot.' He looked at me quizzically. 'You didn't have anything with you, did you. No bags. Clothes?'

'No. I didn't... I wasn't sure where I was coming to. And I didn't know I would be staying either!' I laughed. 'I know that sounds insane. When will your shop be open? There are clothes there, aren't there.'

'Yes. T-shirts, dresses, shorts, swimwear. The grocery store has a selection of boring things, underwear and socks and such. We can start opening any day now. I meant to give Toby a call, actually. She'll probably be in there doing stock ordering around now. So you might get lucky and catch it open. But if not I'll check what time she might be in tomorrow. I can always come down and open up for you. We start getting coaches of day visitors from the city around about now. Retirement home trips, mostly. Sometimes school kids. But they're usually just taken along the forest trail a short way, and back again. Geology lessons or something. Geography. Whatever.'

I finished my cup of tea and added the cup to the dishwasher, thanked Ted again for the breakfast, and took my leave. I didn't return to the caravan, but headed left, out towards the road.

As I walked down the hill I combed my hair with my fingers and occasionally slowed down to stretch my arms into the air and twist my body from side to side. I loved the smell of the air. It was the sea, I supposed, but also the grasses and flowers. An orange car passed me going down into the village. On a balcony of one of the gated properties directly on the main road, I could see a couple, perhaps eating breakfast. Seeing me notice them, the woman raised her hand and waved. I waved back and smiled. She said something to the man with her. They were far out of my earshot, but I could imagine she was wondering aloud who I was. Look at that old woman, I wonder who she is. I haven't seen her before. And he would respond, after glancing in my direction, No, dear, I haven't seen her before, either.

I went directly to the grocery store. The doors slid open automatically and I walked into that familiar atmosphere, crisp and clean and fresh. A gentle, unalarming beep alerted the shopkeeper to the presence of someone entering the store.

'Hello,' said the man behind the counter, cheerfully, before returning to his newspaper.

I took a basket and wandered up and down the aisles looking at all the tins and packets. Many of them familiar names, plenty not. On my trips back to the city since leaving for the forest, I had never lingered for long. I'd known what I wanted and the aim had always been to get in and out in as short a time as possible. Now I found myself mesmerized by the world I had become so detached from. I didn't see the need to start spending money on food. Perhaps I would just get a few tins of soup, a box of cereal, just to look normal in case anyone were to visit me. And I did want tea. There were tins of chocolate powder too. I put one into my basket.

Along with my few food items, I picked up a few pairs of cotton underwear. I lingered on the socks for a while but considering that I'd already left my boots behind at the caravan and was now barefoot, I thought the single pair I'd worn here would probably suffice. Then I went to the counter. The man put down his paper at my approach. He was in his early forties, with dark hair and eyes, and dressed smartly in a shirt and tie. On the fingers of his tanned hands, he wore several silver rings.

'Hi,' I smiled.

'Good morning!' He began taking my things out of the basket and entering prices into the cash register. 'And how are you today? On a day trip? No, you must be staying for a while, to be buying cereal!'

'I am. Are you Percy?'

'That's me! Did you want a bag? So who has been talking about me then?'

'Oh, yes, please. Ted, from the campground, was telling me who's who in the village.'

Percy took a paper bag from beneath the counter and passed it to me.

'I'm going to be doing the cleaning up there, actually.'

'Are you? Oh, well, welcome then. Pleased to make your acquaintance.' He winked at me.

Percy finished totalling up my purchases and held the machine out to me for payment.

'Thank you,' I said.

'Thank *you*. And nice to meet you.'

'You as well. Bye now.'

He tipped an imaginary hat and returned to his newspaper.

I spent the rest of that day sitting on the beach. With my bag of shopping beside my on the sand I settled myself, legs outstretched in front of me, with my back against a large rock.

The ocean receded and returned, and as it came up to the high tide line I could hear it whispering words: come here, come here, come here...

I closed my eyes and listened. It was the land it spoke to, so seductively. It was the rocks who it wanted to break down into sand. It was the shore who it wanted to erode. It wasn't speaking to me. The ocean wasn't even aware of my existence. I was too small, too fleeting. I was the most transient collection of atoms, compared to the lastingness of rock. The pebbles clattered as the surf drew them deeper. Even rock couldn't remain unchanged. The ocean was patient in its surety. Time was on its side.

That night, as I fell asleep, I could still hear it in my mind.

Come here, come here, come here...

And with one foot in dreamland, the other still on waking soil, the voice of the ocean spoke on many levels. It called to all who knew how to listen, and "here" was not a physical place but a way of thinking. Come here... to where time is irrelevant. Come here... to where separation doesn't exist. Come here, come deep, to where you can understand, just for a short while, until you choose to forget, again.

Over the next few weeks I witnessed the village in motion. The strange sunlit quiet, the sleepy haze I had arrived to, it was but one mood of Land's Edge. Another was windows of houses open so that curtains flapped in the breeze, happy squeals of children on the beach blending with the screams of gulls who flocked about, watching keenly the visitors who carried burgers from the van, fish and chips wrapped in paper, ice-cream cones, all of which had a chance of being dropped, if the gulls were lucky. Often I had to stand in line at The Rolling Waves, which I didn't mind at all as I liked to listen to the murmured conversations of couples and families as they considered what they would order.

'Hey, Jetaru,' Dice grinned, as I made it to the counter. 'Usual?'

'Yes please,' I nodded. I had started drinking coffee if I came in before lunch. I had always been a tea drinker but this felt like some kind of experiment with myself.

'How are you today?' I asked.

'Rushed off my feet! And this isn't even what we call busy. But it feels like it after a long quiet winter.' He handed me my drink. 'Yeffie was in this morning to help make up the sandwiches. She'll be back this afternoon. By June I'll be in the swing of things again.'

I took my drink over to my favourite seat by the window and settled down to gaze out at the beach. The tide was out and the sand was dotted with groups of people. I sipped my coffee and thought about how afterwards I would go down and walk across the sand, and walk along the waterline up to my ankles. Just the thought of it was incredibly inviting. Suddenly, a man sat down at my table.

'Hi,' he said. His eyes were hazel, his hair tangled, sun-bleached blonde streaks amongst curls the colour of brown sugar. He was wearing a long-sleeved t-shirt, which looked as if it had started out green but was now bleached so pale that it was almost colourless, and black jeans. He wasn't wearing shoes.

'You're Jetaru,' he said.

'I am.'

'The fishermen were talking about you.' His eyes sparkled with focused merriment. 'My name is Jeremy.'

'Oh, hello Jeremy. I've heard about you, too.'

'Of course you have. People love to talk about people. If you'd met me first, you wouldn't know anyone yet.'

I wondered what the fishermen had said about me but I didn't ask. For some reason I felt ever so slightly shy. Perhaps it was just that I found him very handsome. More than that, I found him attractive. It wasn't something I was used to. I looked out of the window again, then back to him, and laughed.

'I want to hear more about you, Jetaru,' he said, eyes fixed on my face. 'You sound very interesting.'

I think I actually blushed.

'Do I?' I took a sip from my coffee in an attempt to hide that I didn't know what to say.

'Mm-hm. Have you walked along the coast path past The Mermaid yet?'

'No. I've begun cleaning at Ted's campground. There aren't many people staying yet so it hasn't been too bad, but I still need to check it twice a day. The second cleaner will be arriving before the end of this week so I'll have days off, or at least only have to do once a day. It depends what they want to do, I guess. I'm waiting until I don't have to think about the time to explore further than the village.'

Jeremy nodded.

'Well, when you do, come and find me out that way, maybe. I think you will be able to.'

I wasn't sure what he meant by that but he was rising from his seat and I didn't ask, I just watched him stand.

'Seeya later, Jetaru!'

And with that he sauntered towards the cafe door, dropping what I thought must be a coin into the tip jar on the counter and winking at Dice as he passed. After he was gone I watched Dice retrieve the "coin" and hold it up for me to see, rolling his eyes with a grin. It was not a coin, but a very pretty pebble.

The tide was still far enough back that I could walk down onto the sand through the harbour, past the boats where they rested, the mooring chains strung between them.

I walked along the length of the beach, my feet being alternately covered and then uncovered by the lapping water. The midday sun was hot, and when I reached the rocks at the end of the beach furthest from the harbour I sat down, glancing about. There was nobody close enough to really see. I had bought a few items of clothing from Ted's shop and was wearing a pair of knee-length pink swimming shorts with a large white t-shirt. On the t-shirt was an orange octopus above blue lettering that said "Land's Edge". The other t-shirt I'd bought had a tree on it and said "I walked Land's Edge Forest Trail". Along with a sea green cardigan and a spare pair of shorts, as well as the dress I had arrived in, I felt I now had an adequate wardrobe.

I slipped the t-shirt over my head and draped it over the rock I'd been sitting on, then quickly waded out so that my back was to anyone who might look my way. The bay was calm, the sea still and brilliantly clear. Looking down I could see my feet, the image wavering through the water. The sun burned hot on my shoulders, and when I was up to my waist I crouched down until it came to my neck. I lay back, letting myself float. My ears submerged, salt water rushing into them, and I closed my eyes automatically. Then I opened them, letting them fill with the blue of the sky as my ears filled with the sound of the underwater. How could something be like both a whisper and a roar? How could it sound so close, and so distant? Faraway underwater vibrations... how far? How far?

And although the sea was calm, now that I was in it I could feel the sway. I could feel the push and pull. For a long time I lay in the water experiencing this new sensation. Until that point, in over a thousand years, I had never been in a body of water bigger than a bathtub. This was not the same. I stretched out my arms and moved them about. For such a while did I lose myself in this activity, that when I turned to look back at where I'd left my t-shirt, I noticed that the water was now surrounding that rock. I returned to retrieve it, crossing my arms over my chest self-consciously, and pulled it on over my damp skin. Water dripped down my legs from my shorts. Neither would take long to dry, I thought. On my way back to the campground, I stopped in the doorway of Ted's shop to say hello to Toby.

Her name was October Sunshine but nobody called her that. Her eyes were light brown, seemingly golden against her brown skin, and her hair was bleached blonde, cut to shoulder length and decorated with a rainbow of coloured beads at the end of many tiny plaits. She was twenty-five and had been living in Land's Edge since she was nineteen. When she caught sight of me at the doorway, she beamed.

'Hi! How's it going? Your hair is wet. Did you go in the sea?'

'The first time I've ever done it,' I nodded.

'Awesome! Yeah, I feel super sorry for the people who never come to the coast. The dome pools don't come close. There is nothing like ocean swimming.'

'Have you been busy today?'

'Not really. Never are when it's low tide around midday like this. They all want to be on the beach. Until July, August, then it's busy all day usually. You have a few campers now, right? How's it going up there?'

'Not bad. The other cleaner arrives tomorrow. She's eighteen, apparently. Um. I've forgotten what Ted said her name was. I'm looking forward to having some days off for exploring.'

'Right! You have to do the forest trail! So that your t-shirt isn't a lie.' Toby grinned.

'Absoutely,' I agreed.

'If you need to borrow anything when you do that, I can lend you. Like a backpack? Sleeping bag. Stuff like that.'

'That's kind of you.'

'No problem.'

A middle-aged couple came past me into the shop, smiling at me and nodding to Toby's cheerful greeting. They began the usual shuffling circuit around the shelves, murmuring over the ornaments and fridge magnets, pointing out the attractive stoneware with the starfish design. At the postcard rack the woman began picking out cards.

'I'd better get going. I'll see you soon, Toby.'

'Yep. Seeya soon Jetaru. Oh, hey, there's a band playing at The Mermaid this Saturday, friends of mine from the city actually. You'll come along, right?'

'Absolutely. I haven't been in there yet. I met Charlie on the beach one morning.'

'They're fun people, Erin and Charlie. And Erin makes the best pies.'

'What's your friend's band like?'

'Ummm... Hard to describe. Like, um, ethereal. Kinda jazz. Dance rock vibes. They're called Sugar Lizard.'

'Okay. I'm intrigued.' I thought about how long it had been since I'd even listened to music at all, other than my own singing. A long while. 'Well, if not before, I'll see you there!'

'Seeya!'

The second cleaner was a studious young girl called Josie who wore pink-framed glasses with thick lenses that magnified her blue eyes. Right away I noticed her tag, which rarely left the palm of her hand although was occasionally slipped into a back pocket. She had just finished school and was planning to start training as a nurse after the summer. She would sit on the step of her caravan with a stack of text books, alternating her attention between her studies and the little round screen.

We agreed to split the cleaning by day rather than shift, with her doing Saturday afternoon, Sunday, Monday and Tuesday while I took Wednesday to Friday and Saturday morning. Unlike Toby, who treated everyone pretty much the same whether they were eight or eighty, I could feel a definite wall between Josie and I. It was apparent that she saw me as an old woman. This was more mildly amusing than upsetting; it didn't matter to me that her tone became considered and polite when she spoke to me, or that she'd exclaimed that I had such good legs *for my age*. The last time I had interacted with the rest of society so closely, I had been young. How strange to be treated so differently, almost as if I were a small child, all because my body had aged. Had I done the same when I was a teenager?

On Saturday I went to The Mermaid earlier than I'd planned to for the music. It was only a little past three in the afternoon but clouds had come over, and though it was warm a light drizzle had begun. Also, I wanted to try one of the esteemed pies.

It hadn't gone unnoticed by me that even in the short time I had been here, just a little over a month, appetites had been awoken in my heart and stomach. For food, company, and even the stimulation of playing video games with Ted. None of it was necessary but neither did there seem any reason not to indulge my physical senses and hungers after so long spent mostly in my own mind.

Three fishermen sat at the bar. I recognised Wilson, and beside him was a small, wiry man with bright red hair.

On the other side of him sat a younger man, perhaps in his mid-twenties. Both of these two I'd noticed in passing but I didn't know their names. They all looked around when I came in.

'It's the crazy lady,' Wilson said, loudly enough for it to be for my benefit. There was no unkindness in his voice, but neither did he smile.

'Hi, Crazy Lady,' grinned the flame-headed man. He turned on his stool and stuck out his hand. 'I'm Rooster.'

I came to meet him and shook his hand.

'Jetaru,' I told him.

'That's Orion,' he told me, pointing with his thumb at the youngest member of their group.

'Hi Orion.'

'Hey,' he responded in a soft voice. I recalled that this was the young man who Ted had told me was in love with Eloise.

Then Charlie appeared from the back room and sauntered down behind the bar to us, her wild tumble of black curls tied up in a messy bun above her round face, black denim dungarees with one shoulder strap unfastened, bikini top underneath.

'Same again, boys?' she asked the fishermen, and was met with grunts that signalled the affirmative. She began refilling their glasses and looked at me. 'Hello again. Jetaru, right? What can I get you?'

'A lemonade, thanks. With ice.'

'Right you are!'

'And I've heard a lot about these famous pies...'

'We'll have a first batch of pies ready in about half an hour. Here's a menu. My Sweet is just putting them into the oven about now. Or, about ten minutes ago. She'll be jumping in the shower about now. So I might just leave you all to it for a short while!' She winked, and scooped ice into my lemonade. Just then the door opened and a woman with a feather in her hat and carrying part of a drum kit looked in.

'Hi! We're playing here tonight?'

'Yes! Come on in, dudes!' Charlie lowered her voice and said, for our benefit, 'Ah well. Gonna miss that shower, I guess.'

'I can always go and check on Erin if you want, Char,' joked Rooster. Charlie rolled her eyes and went to help the band who were bringing in more equipment.

'Here, we'll set you up over here on this raised section. Our stage. We just need to move these two small tables. They can fit in over on that side. Yep, that's right. Stack a few of the chairs and just shove them in this corner.'

I seated myself on the stool beside Rooster and sipped my lemonade while scanning the menu Charlie had given me. There were six different pies on the pink sheet of paper, and the option of a bowl of potato wedges.

'So how are you finding life here, Jay?' asked Rooster.

'Oh, I just look for it each morning,' I replied. This elicited an unexpected laugh from Wilson. 'I'm enjoying it,' I added. 'It's a really nice place.'

'Nicer when it's not overrun,' muttered Wilson.

'But the ladies, Willie! The ladies!'

Wilson shrugged dismissively.

'Oh, you get me, right Ori? We like seeing all the summer ladies, don't we.'

'Sure.'

'Ah get out. Like you have heart eyes for anyone except–'

'Shut up, Wil,' Orion interrupted.

They began talking about fishing and their morning's catches, and my attention wandered to the band who were now all inside with their instruments, setting things up on the low stage, plugging in wires, checking their tuning. There were seven of them and they were a colourful group. There were two women and the others were men. Most of them looked around Toby's age but one of the women and one of the men appeared somewhat older, perhaps about forty. The words "Sugar Lizard" had been hand-painted on a banner that they pinned up on the wall behind the instruments.

Erin appeared behind the bar wearing a white mini dress, her long blonde hair still damp.

'Hey, Beautiful,' greeted Rooster.

'Sup, Dumbass,' responded Erin, but there was a twinkle in her eye. 'So can I take anyone's order for a pie?'

'Yup,' said Wilson, slapping his hand on the bar for emphasis. 'Usual. Fish.'

'Same,' added Orion.

Rooster gave a thumbs up, in response to Erin's questioning eyebrow raise. Then she looked at me.

'Roast vegetable, please,' I told her.

'Three fish, one vegetable. Hey! You guys,' she called to the band; 'any of you want pies? Fish, roast vegetable, sweet potato, broccoli 'n cheese, steak, lamb?'

They began calling choices back and Erin began scribbling them down on a scrap of paper.

The pies were as good as everyone had told me. Within the hour the bar had begun to fill with people. The locals tended to congregate around the bar whilst visitors sat at the tables in their own groups. Some from each side of the divide knew each other and these bantered and laughed, while quieter families watched with big round eyes. There were a few children running around and when

Toby arrived she traded high fives with them as if they were old friends.

Then the band assembled and began to play. Around me the volume of the conversation increased and Toby motioned with her eyes towards the stage. I nodded and smiled, and we made our way closer. After the first song one of the men, a violinist with dark make-up around his eyes, came to the microphone and thanked Erin and Charlie for having them a second year running.

'And now we'd like to dedicate this next song to our good friend, Toby,' he added, beaming our way. 'She's the reason we ever found our way out here in the first place!'

'Woooo-OOH!' Toby yelled back at them.

And with that they launched into a fast-paced whirling dance that made it impossible for anyone to stand still. I was tapping my feet and clapping my hands together, and suddenly Percy had his arm around my shoulder, laughing and pulling me into the room. He was still dressed in his smart clothes, but his tie was loose and his shirt sleeves were rolled up, and it was clear that he loved to dance. He appeared to be good friends with Dice who tonight was wearing another brightly coloured scarf around his head, this one green and purple. The two men were having great fun stamping their feet and pulling the shyer dancers onto the floor.

At some point I noticed a young woman, still seated, but from the excitement in her eyes it was obvious that she was enjoying the music as much as any of the dancers. Her hair was very pale, with a silvery hue, and on each wrist she wore several silver bangles. She was dressed in a pale grey silk shirt, and wide-legged loose trousers that matched. Toby noticed me noticing her.

'That's Eloise,' she leaned close to tell me. 'She hasn't opened shop yet but she will very soon. The first of June, probably. She doesn't go out a lot. She stays at home, above the shop. She has a work room right at the top under the sloping roof. Did you notice the big round window? Hardly anyone has been invited up there, or in her home at all.'

'You have?'

'Yep,' she smiled, proudly.

I looked around, seeking out Orion. Sure enough he was positioned on a stool near the bar where he could easily see her, and every now and then he would glance in her direction. The look on his face was such a blend of pain and ecstasy that I had to smile. I wondered why he didn't declare his feelings to her.

'Hey, this is Yeffie! Have you guys met?'

My attention was brought around to a girl with chestnut brown hair tied back into a pony tail. Behind her, I recognised Gilly and an older man who had Gilly's arm.

'Hi! No, we haven't. Hi Yeffie.'

'Hey. Nice to meet you. Dice told me a little about you. You're cleaning at Ted's, right?'

'Yes. You work for Dice in the cafe. I've admired your sandwich talents.'

'Oh, yes. I am a creative genius when it comes to sandwiches,' Yeffie grinned. 'I do quite a lot of cleaning in the holiday homes, too.'

'Hello again Jetaru,' Gilly said. 'This is my husband, Giles. Honey, this is the woman I told you about? The one who stopped to say hello to Seeker.'

'Ah!' Memory lit up his face. 'Ah, yes. My pleasure, Maam.' And he took my hand, kissing it. 'Now, my love,' he addressed his wife, 'are we going to have a dance?'

'Of course we are! Yeffie, honey, would you get us some drinks? You know I can't handle the bar when it's this busy.'

'Sure, mother.'

And the two old farmers, hand in hand, joined the merry atmosphere on the dance floor.

That evening I met several people I had not already met. Wilson's wife, Hannah, was amongst them. She was dark skinned, full of laughter, and wore yellow. At first I thought her a surprising match for Wilson, but it wasn't long before I saw how well they balanced each other. She told me that she often couldn't come out to nights like these as they had two young children, a twelve and ten year old. It turned out that Josie was earning some extra money babysitting them.

It was an entirely enjoyable night, although I noticed in my heart a slight disappointment not to meet Jeremy again, here. Ted had arrived late, having driven down the hill, and at half-past midnight when it was time to go home I was glad of the ride. As I fell asleep in my caravan I decided that tomorrow I must head out along the coast path to Distant Point.

I slept later than usual after my one-in-the-morning bedtime. The sun was already up but there was a haze in the sky which reminded me of my first day here. I dressed in my shorts and Forest Trail t-shirt, and after a quick consideration of my boots I left without them. I hadn't worn them since I'd arrived, but of course I hadn't been further out of the village. Carrying out my ritual I splashed my face with water, drank from my cupped hands, and then set off down the hill.

I crossed the parking lot, past the closed doors of The Mermaid, and stopped for a moment at the head of the trail. There was a small sign on a post which read:

Coastpath – Distant Point 4.5 miles.

Sometimes, from where I was standing, the point was visible, but on this morning the haze obscured the view. I began walking.

The path wound gently upwards between rocks and orange-blossomed bushes until the sea was far beneath me, hidden by the mist. Tiny pink flowers were dotted across the grass, which sloped away from the other side of the path, towards the forest. The mist enveloped me, and I couldn't see more than a few metres ahead. It felt as though I were walking a path through the sky, amongst the clouds.

After a while the path began to descend again. The sea came back into view through the mist, foamy water swelling up and down around the rocks. It wasn't long before I was back at sea level where the path merged into a beach of course sand. Away from the water, rock-strewn heath land sloped upwards to the forest edge about a quarter of a mile away. Then the beach ended in boulders while the path continued just above them on the flat, springy coastal grass.

The wind had picked up and was blowing in quite hard, but it wasn't cold. There were spits of rain, or maybe that was just spray from the sea. I continued on. Finally the path began to curve to the right and I realised I must now be heading out towards the point. I left the path and climbed up the bank of wild meadow, curious to see the lay of the land. Yes, when I looked from up here, I could see over to the sea lapping at the other side of the low peninsula I stood on, but there was no path on that side. The path would end out ahead of me, surrounded by the sea. I looked back along the coast the way I had come. On a clear day I'd have been able to see the village in the distance. Not that day. I returned to the path and kept on until I reached the end. The meadow soon disappeared, and the path ran along the top of the narrow spit of land so I could look down to the sea either side. It occurred to me that in a storm this would be a dangerous place to be. When I had gone as far as I could go I found myself standing in a circle of boulders. There was a small metal plaque screwed onto one of them which said:

Distant Point. Land's Edge Village 4.5 miles.

The might-be-rain-might-be-sea-spray became definite rain and I started retracing my steps. But this time, now that I was looking in the right direction, I noticed that if I were to climb down the other side of my look out point I'd be on a small rocky beach. And nestled amongst the boulders in the grass above it I could see some kind of structure. And there was a thin column of smoke rising from it, being quickly snatched away by the wind.

It was not an easy climb down and the rain didn't make it any better, but I managed to reach the beach. Later on I would learn the route Jeremy took around the back of his hut; a secret path that ran above the official path before coming so close that even though it was hidden from view by the tall grasses, you could scramble from one to the other.

As I got closer I could see that the structure was a small hut constructed like a child's den out of driftwood, old rope, and other pieces of debris that I presumed had been thrown up by the sea. The roof was a patchwork of corrugated iron, tarpaulin, and a small wooden boat, upside down and clearly no longer sea-worthy. A kind of sheltered veranda wrapped around two sides of the hut and there was a window looking out to sea. I wondered if my approach was being observed.

'Jeremy?' I called out, tentatively. The door was on the sheltered side, and just as I was about to knock, it opened.

'Jetaru,' smiled Jeremy. 'Come in! What a day!' And he ushered me inside, closing the door.

Inside, the hut was not what I expected from having seen the outside. The walls had been carefully panelled with driftwood, and there was an armchair in one corner. Shelves on the walls held books, along with beautiful shells, rocks, and some kind of clock in a brass casing. There was a wood-burning stove in another corner giving the room its cosy warmth. A metal tub hung by one of its handles on a hook on the wall. Then finally what caught my attention was a computer on a desk against the wall. I looked at the ceiling; there was no light fitting. And the candle stubs around the place testified to this. How surprising that there would be a computer. I wondered if it would even turn on. There was no other sign of electricity.

'You're wet. Sit by the fire. Here,' he pulled the chair across the room so it was closer to the stove, 'sit down, please. I'll put the kettle on.'

And with that he took a large copper kettle from a hook, disappeared outside, and then returned with the kettle evidently filled. He placed it on the stove and came to sit on the floor. Then he just looked up at me for a long moment. Finally, he spoke.

'So, where are you from, Jetaru?' he said.

'I was born in the city, and grew up there,' I answered.

'Hm. Of course. Where else.' He raised an eyebrow. 'But that isn't where you are from.'

I laughed, thinking of where I was really from.

'What's funny?'

'Oh, nothing.'

'You're used to hiding the truth from people. You're used to people that you have to hide the truth from.'

'I don't hide anything,' I said.

'What do you think is on the other side of the water?' he asked, changing the subject. He looked out of the window at the sea.

'Why, nothing. It's infinite, of course. Everyone knows that.' But I gave him a look as I said this, and added: 'Infinite, like the forest.'

'You think there's something on the other side of the forest?'

'If there is, I've never found it.'

'Have you tried to find it?'

'Well. I've spent a lot of time in the forest.'

'That's unusual,' said Jeremy, turning to look at me.

'Yep. I've gone far enough into the forest to know it's all identical, past a certain point.' I'd never ventured this information to anyone else.

'I walked along the coast once,' said Jeremy. 'Not in this direction, the other way. The beach in that direction just goes on and on. I never reached an end.'

'I'm not really used to people, at all.' I returned to his earlier statement. Then I changed the subject myself. 'Does that computer work?'

'Yes.'

The kettle began to boil and Jeremy stood, went over and took two cups down from another shelf, and also a box of tea. He spooned tea into a large green teapot and paused, waiting while it brewed.

The computer was quite big and boxy. It reminded me of computers from when I was in school. It would have been old-fashioned even by the time I left the city, let alone now.

'How do you... how does it run? You have electricity?' I looked about.

Jeremy laughed, went over to the desk, and pulled the wooden stool out of the way. I could see now that wires were running down from the back of the computer and through a crack in the floor. Jeremy pulled up a floorboard and motioned for me to come and look.

'See? This is a battery, here. The wires there that go off away from the house, they go to a water turbine in a stream that runs down from the hills but goes underground before it reaches the sea.'

'You built all this? It's impressive.'

Jeremy shrugged. He fetched the cups of tea and handed one to me, before sitting back down with his own. I sat back down on the armchair.

'Not really. It only seems complicated when you don't know how it works. I learned slowly. I have a book about it all, up there.' He pointed to his bookshelf. 'So how come you're not used to people?'

I took a deep breath, sipped my tea, then looked out of the window. I was so accustomed to my secret existence. But my intuition said that the time for truth was now. That, finally, I had come across someone who wouldn't think I was crazy, and might even understand.

'Until my thirty-third year of this life, I lived in the city. In the house I'd grown up in. My parents both died in my late twenties. I was working at a payment centre.' I paused, unsure of how to explain the next part.

'This life,' Jeremy murmured. Not questioning.

'Things had been... strange... for a while. I needed to focus. I was having a lot of dreams. I had this idea that I would find what I was looking for in the forest. So I went. And I lived there. I've been living there ever since, until I came here.'

'How?'

'You mean how did I shelter? I found a cabin. A wooden cabin. There was a woodstove in there. A few other things, a saw. A wheelbarrow. Nothing much else. I brought a few things with me, and I went back to the city every few years to fetch supplies.'

Jeremy raised his eyebrows and whistled.

'Well now. I knew you were interesting. Well. What a story. I'll have to think about this. Do you know where the cabin came from? Do you know who built it? Was it long abandoned when you found it?'

I shook my head.

'I don't know anything about why it's there. It didn't seem like anyone had been there for a long time. But it wasn't dilapidated, either.'

The rain was coming down harder now, blurring the world through the glass.

'How did you get that window here?' I asked.

'With a lot of hard work!' Jeremy laughed. 'And very slowly. One of the panes got broken. I had to replace it once it was here.'

'And what about you? Why do you live out here?'

'I just like to be alone and I like to be close to the ocean. I don't know. I liked building dens all my life. When we were kids, Gilly and me, that's my sister–'

'Yes, I've met her.'

'–we used to build dens together all the time. On the beach, in the forest. Sometimes we'd camp out on them, even. And I suppose I just never grew up. My den building has improved though!'

He stood up and went to a small chest.

'Do you play chess?' he asked, opening the chest.

I shook my head.

'I've never learned. It looked complicated.'

'Nah.' Jeremy shook his head and grinned. 'Only when you don't know how. I'll teach you.'

And for the rest of that day that is what he did. It didn't take me long to understand the rules of how each piece could move, but I could tell it would take a while longer to really develop an understanding of strategy. We spoke very little, and of nothing besides the game. In the late afternoon the rain cleared. I knew I should start back or else I would risk not making it back before dark. Jeremy made me take his flashlight just in case, assuring me that I could bring it back another day.

On my way back along the highest clifftop part of the path, I could now see clearly. The view was as I had imagined. The dark blue, cold sea was far below me to my left, and to my right I could see across the top of the forest. The sun was setting, turning the top of the canopy into a golden-green carpet that went on and on and on.

When I reached the end of the trail and came out beside The Mermaid it was dusk, and the first stars were visible. I was glad to have the flashlight, although I found I didn't need it for the last stretch up the road to the campground. I fell asleep very quickly, exhausted by the long walk. I knew I wouldn't make it again tomorrow. But maybe the day after, I pondered dreamily, before disappearing into wherever it is we go when we sleep.

The next day I spent an hour hanging out with Toby in the shop. We had mugs of hot chocolate from the cafe and I perched on a stool near the counter, watching the people and enjoying the warm breeze coming in through the door. Kites swooped up and down, being flown from the beach, bright colours against the blue sky with fluttering tails of ribbons. People in the shop quietly murmured to one another, some silently contemplated items on the shelves. Two women giggled as they tried on hats. Every so often Toby would tap numbers into the til, each button beeping its own note, and she gave it rhythm, making it music. Ka-ching, and the cash drawer would spring open, and then she pushed it back so it closed with a metallic click.

Toby had a talent for keeping her awareness spread wide so that she knew the moment she was needed, to make a sale or give advice, offer help or refill the postcard rack. And still I felt she was present with me; we chatted while she presided over her kingdom.

'Toby, do you have a tag?'

'Sure. It's here.' And she produced the familiar disk from her bag on the floor. 'I mostly just use it to stay in contact with friends who live in the city. I do that on the Call app though. I don't have a Livetime account, or ShowMe, or any of those kinds of things.

'Well, I used to have ShowMe, when I lived back there. It just took up so much *time,* dude. And I didn't seem to be able to control that. Like, I'd decide to only scroll for an hour a day and stick to that for a week but then I'd start spending longer, and I could never make the good habit stick. Or I'd decide not to even open the app on every other day but taking it away just made me feel the addiction. My thumb would just like, go to open the app without me even thinking about it. Seriously!

'So when I moved here I just thought, to hell with it, and deleted it all. It was way easier because I was meeting new people and starting this job, and almost no-one here is on any of that stuff so no-one talks about it. Once it wasn't there, I barely even missed it. How about you? I'm betting you don't even have a tag, right?'

'Right,' I nodded. There was a break in our conversation while Toby served two children who were each buying an assortment of beaded and woven bracelets.

'Apparently there wasn't even signal for tags out here anyway, until the arcade was built, only, uh, two years, I think, before I arrived. People used computers via the phone line, so I guess they could plug tags into that if they wanted, but no-one's going to have a tag only to use it plugged into a computer, are they. I guess they needed to install it in the arcade to control the robot. It's open now, have you seen it yet?'

'A robot?'

'Yeah. I guess you haven't then. You'd know. It walks around up and down in front of the building, talking to people. Encouraging them to go inside, wishing them a good day, that kind of thing.'

'Is it intelligent?'

'Not sure,' Toby shrugged. 'I think so, some kind of simple learning algorithm or something. The older fishermen might tell you it's just remote controlled, but they don't really understand how advanced technology in the city has become. I mean, most of them have lived their entire lives out here. Kind of blissful, really.'

When I left the shop I wandered along to see the robot. As Toby had said it would be, it was marching up and down on the raised step in front of the arcade. It was a couple of feet taller than me, with a silver square-edged body and a head like an old television set. The eyes, a collection of tiny blue lights which blinked and pulsed in various patterns to give the appearance of expression, turned to me as I approached.

'HI THERE!'

'Um, hi,' I replied.

'ARE YOU GOING TO COME IN AND PLAY?'

'I don't think so, not today.'

'OH. VERY WELL! PERHAPS ANOTHER DAY!'

'Yes. Perhaps.'

'I ENJOY WATCHING THE PEOPLE PLAY.'

A line of pink lights which simulated a mouth, blinking in time with the robot's words, arranged themselves into a smile. I couldn't help but find it quite endearing.

'I'm on my way to sit on the harbour for a while, Robot,' I said. 'It's too nice to be indoors. I'll come and play when it's raining again.'

'THAT IS A SWELL IDEA!' agreed the robot. 'SEE YOU ON A RAINY DAY THEN.'

'Yes, see you on a rainy day,' I replied, and walked on.

Mel and Kurt's food truck was parked at the top of the harbour in the turning circle. It was painted a cheerful orange, with blue and pink lettering along the side that said *Brilliant Burgers (+fries!)*. A trio of seagulls stood on the roof, watching keenly. I hadn't yet met these people, so I sidled up to the window. A couple who were waiting for their order smiled at me.

'Hey there!' A face I would have placed at around forty, with straight, dark hair tied up in a messy bun, and kind, hazel eyes, appeared and greeted me. 'What can I get you?'

'Hi! Oh, I'll have just a fries, please. I wanted to say hello, too. My name is Jetaru. I'm working at–'

'Oh hi, Jetaru! Yes we've heard about you. You're up at Ted's, right?'

'That's right,' I nodded.

'Word gets around in a small place like this.' She turned to call into the van, 'Kurt, love? One fries! It's Jetaru, the woman Charlie was telling us about.'

A second face appeared at the window. Kurt grinned at me with white teeth, stubble on brown cheeks. His face was broad and friendly.

'Nice to meet you, Jetaru!' And with that he was gone again. A moment later he returned with two cardboard boxes and called to the waiting couple. 'Here you go!'

The woman smiled at me as her husband took the food.

'These are the best burgers! We come here every year. We've had almost everything on the menu!'

I glanced at the menu beside the serving window. There were indeed a great variety of options. Besides fries, the only thing they provided was burgers, but so many different kinds! A good number of them were not meat, too. Killing and eating other animals has always seemed messy, uneconomical, and a little gross, to me.

'Here you go, Jetaru!' Kurt returned to the window with my fries. 'Keep your hand over them. Watch out for those damn gulls.'

'So how are you enjoying life here?' asked Mel.

'I love it,' I replied. 'I've never been in the sea before, that's a completely new pleasure to me.'

'Oh, yes,' said Mel. 'I'm a big believer in the magical properties of saltwater. I swim every morning, every day of the year.'

'And look how beautiful it keeps her!' added Kurt, giving his wife a warm look.

'Oh stop,' she laughed, batting away the words with her hand.

'Maybe I could join you some time?' I asked.

'You absolutely could! Oh, please do. I would love that. It's usually just around sunrise, or a little after.'

A group of three couples all approached the van, eyeing the menu.

'Okay! I'm usually up pretty early.' I stepped aside to let the group forward. 'See you soon.'

I walked on down to the harbour, eating my fries and keeping a protective hand cupped over them as Kurt had warned me to do. At the end of the quay were several large containers of nets, as well as lobster pots and various sizes of pink, green and orange buoys. There were several other people sitting along the wall, some of them also eating. Gulls watched, threw back their heads, and called into the sky. The tide had come in a little way but the boats were not yet floating. Children paddled between them.

I walked back up and along the road until I was outside Silver & Stone. It was open now and I could see Eloise inside, seated beside her small counter. I opened the door and a little bell tinkled. Eloise looked up from the book she was reading and smiled at me with obvious recognition.

'Hello, Jetaru. I've heard so much about you, but we haven't been properly introduced. I'm Eloise Feyton.' She held out her hand, prettily.

I came over and took it.

'Jetaru Dark.'

I glanced around at the shop. It was beautifully arranged, with sun-bleached branches of driftwood and large, smooth, grey pebbles artfully placed. Resting on the pebbles and hanging from the wood were all of Eloise's creations. The wooden seagulls, suspended from the ceiling, moved in the breeze coming through the door.

'What a gorgeous little shop you have,' I said.

'Thank you.'

I began a slow circuit, letting my eyes wander over her displays.

'I saw you dancing at The Mermaid,' she said. 'Wasn't it a wonderful night?'

'It was,' I agreed. 'It's been a long time since I've danced!'

'Me too,' she murmured. 'I get very tired, very quickly,' she added.

'Ah.'

'I've seen doctors, in the city. But they never find anything wrong. They just advise me to rest. To eat more spinach.' She laughed.

'I've never heard of Otherside.'

'It's where I'm from,' she said, a touch of pride in her voice. 'Not many people grow up there. Most people go back to the city to raise a family. Not many folk bring their children up in Quarrytown.

'Otherside is all the way back along the road to the city, and then you carry on and go just as far, a bit further, in the other direction. Then you reach the other coast. First, through the mountains, and then the coast. It's different than this side. It's jagged and big, and the sky is sharper. There isn't all the farm land like there is here. There are many different quarry sites and in the middle of them is Quarrytown, and the road out. It's a lively place to grow up in.'

'When did you come here?'

'Oh, a little over nine years ago. I spent a some time in the city, a couple of years. I went to school to learn silversmithing. My dad taught me to carve stone, I've been doing it since I was small. There is nothing to do for work in Quarrytown unless you want to work in the quarries, or cook for the people who do, that's what my mother does, or you marry someone who will keep you. There aren't a lot of women. Most of the men who have families leave them in the city. I didn't want to stay in the city.'

'So you came here.'

'Yes. My grandfather left me an inheritance and that bought me this house. I converted this ground floor into the shop myself.'

'Are your parents still in Quarrytown?'

'Yes. I still go back to Quarrytown to pick out the stones I want to use for my jewellery, myself. I always stay with them then. They don't work so much now, they're getting older, but they have their house and they're happy there. They have friends they've known almost all their lives.'

'It's a really beautiful stone.'

'Sunset stone. That's the name I prefer. I find I work best in the night-time, and often don't go to bed until quite a while after midnight, so I don't see a lot of sunrises. This is a sunrise village though. You can only see the true sunset if you go up the hill. In Quarrytown I love to watch the sun sink into the sea.'

I'd stopped to linger over the tiaras. Each one had a different creature in the centre, carved from the stone. A gull with outstretched wings, a fish, an octopus.

'You like those?' asked Eloise.

I nodded.

'That suits you. You have the aura of a queen.'

'That's a very pleasant compliment,' I said, looking up and feeling a slight blush across my cheeks. 'What's this one?' I asked. 'I don't recognise this animal.'

'Oh, that's a sea otter. I don't think they've ever been seen in the ocean here, but you see them off the coast of Otherside. They're my favourites! They float on their backs and use their own stomachs as a table to eat shellfish off.'

'Wow. Do they make a noise?'

'They whistle!'

I laughed.

'You must come round, sometime. Some evening. I would like to show you my workshop,' said Eloise, suddenly.

'I would be honoured,' I said, remembering what Toby had told me. The invitation surprised and touched me.

'Perhaps in a few weeks? It will be midsummer. October often celebrates with me. You should join us. I would like that.'

'She lets you call her that?'

'She doesn't have a choice,' Eloise replied with a smirk.

'I would be delighted to join you. Thank you.'

At that point, the doorbell tinkled as a couple entered the shop. I took it as my cue to leave, and gave her a soft murmured *goodbye for now* as I slipped out, leaving her to her potential customers.

Before I returned home I went back into Ted's and bought an olive green bathing suit. If I was going to be swimming more often, I wanted to be appropriately dressed.

That evening I played video games with Ted.

'What do you think of the arcade?' I asked him.

'Oh, you met the robot, did you? Yes. I don't mind it, not as much as some of the locals. Obviously I preferred it when there was no tag coverage. But it doesn't really affect me.' He shrugged. 'I try not to spend too much time or energy on things that don't really affect me.'

'Who decides about things like that being built? For the village, I mean. Who is in charge? Do people here vote in the city elections?'

'Yes, we vote in the elections. And the city council are in charge here. It wasn't always like that. We still have a council representative. At the moment it's a woman called Alice. She owns a house here but she doesn't live here full time. Nobody who lives here wants to be going to the city all the time, and they'd have to do that every time there was a meeting that concerned us. This system works alright, in my opinion.'

'Hm.'

'There are definitely a few who would like it to be more independent again. Especially amongst the fishermen. Most of them are descendants of old families who have been here for generations going way, way back. I said we *do* vote in the city elections, but it's more that we *can*. Most of us don't. Most here would probably agree with me when I say elections usually seem to be about giving people the illusion that they have a say in what happens, when really the rich and powerful are going to have their way no matter what. Alice is alright though. She holds meetings at The Mermaid every six months or so, takes on board what people here think, and tries to represent us honestly.'

'Ah, damn,' I cursed as, on the screen, my car went off the track and smashed into a tree.

'Oh nooo,' Ted laughed.

In the end I did not return to Jeremy's hut the following day as I'd thought I might. I woke before sunrise, dressed in my new bathing suit with t-shirt and shorts over it, wrapped a towel around my shoulders, and went down to the village to swim with Mel.

There was a thick layer of cloud overhead but we could see the edge of it out to sea, and the sun shining down creating a strip of glittering water along the horizon. With Mel's company for reassurance I was happy to go much farther from the shore than I had done by myself. The water was so clear. Even well out of my depth I could look down and see the shimmering yellow sand, and the occasional dark shape of rock. We floated for a while. Mel told me about how she and Kurt had come to the village eleven years ago after Kurt's high-paying but intensely stressful job in marketing had brought him close to the edge of a mental breakdown.

'I was teaching kindergartners at the time. I loved it. But I, too, felt that we were missing one of the most important parts of living. We spent far too little time together. My colleagues were all good people, but they were not kindred souls. I didn't want to look back and wonder why I'd spent more of my life with them than with Kurt. When his problems got too bad, that was the tipping point. We decided to sell everything, buy the food truck, and make a new life here. It was somewhere we'd only read about and never even visited!

'It was not as easy as I'm making it sound. There were definitely moments where I wondered what the hell I was doing, whether I was making a huge mistake. We got the trader's licence from the city but we still didn't know how the people here would take to us. The first thing we did was check how Dice and the girls at The Mermaid felt about it, and what food they sold. We made the decision to specialize in burgers since it felt like it wouldn't be stepping on anyone's toes.'

'I'll try one later,' I said. 'The menu looked impressive.'

'Thanks! There was the initial wariness often shown to newcomers in a place like this. But I like to think we fitted in pretty quickly. And it's been home ever since!'

The sun rose higher, passing beyond the gap of clear sky and going behind the cloud. Abruptly it seemed much darker and colder. We swam back to the beach and dried off just as the rain started. Above us on the road a vehicle horn sounded.

'Hey ladies!' Kurt shouted down. 'I guessed the weather was going to catch you! Thought you might like it if I drove down a little early.'

'I like it a lot, my beloved!' Mel called back up to him.

We hurried up the steps.

'I'll go to the cafe for a while,' I said, as Mel climbed into the van. 'Thanks for letting me join you.'

'Same time, any day! I really enjoyed having the company. See you later!'

'Later,' I waved.

In the cafe I bought a hot chocolate and went to sit by the window, enjoying the feeling of being warm and dry behind the glass as rain pelted against it.

'You went out with Mel this morning then,' said Dice, coming over and leaning against the edge of my table.

'Oh, did you see us? Yes. I enjoyed going out into the deep. I'd have been too scared on my own. I'm glad to find someone who knows what they're doing.'

'Aw, she's dedicated alright. I've rarely seen her skip a day. Are you going to make it a regular thing?'

'I think I might, yes.'

The volume of the rain increased briefly as the door opened, the cooler air swirling in around the legs of a pair of walkers dressed in head-to-toe florescent waterproofs.

'Although I might find it harder if the weather were already like this before I headed out,' I added.

'I know I would,' said Dice. 'Mel goes anyway though! Sometimes Kurt drives her down in the van. They're a good couple of people. Solid.' He headed back to the counter to serve the customers.

A minute later the door opened again and Yeffie put her head in.

'Hey Dice. Hey Jetaru! Dice, are you going to need me today, do you think?'

'Ehh...' Dice looked out the window.

'It's fine if you don't! It'll suit me, actually. I had a call from the owners of Beachview, and they want the whole place cleaned. Today! They weren't going to take bookings until July, they told me back in February, but they've changed their minds and there are visitors arriving tomorrow afternoon.'

'Ugh!' Dice exclaimed, with a sympathetic roll of his eyes. 'Yeah, of course, go do that. It's going to be a quiet day. I don't think the rain is easing until much later this afternoon.'

'Thanks, Dice.'

While this conversation was taking place I had wandered over to a small bookshelf in the corner, filled with well-thumbed paperbacks. When Dice said that the rain wasn't going to ease I gave up on the coastal walk to Jeremy's hut, and decided to spend the day reading. Several books caught my eye but the one I picked up had a plain white cover and was titled in metallic gold lettering:

A Question of God

I turned it over to read the blurb on the back cover.

On a park bench, a series of colourful characters come and go, each picking up the thread of a continuous conversation exploring the nature of who or what God is.

I flipped through the pages and found that it was written as a play. I'd never developed any strong opinions about religion. It seemed perfectly obvious to me that if there were such a thing as a god, it would surely be beyond our comprehension, and that anyone who thought they comprehended it was lying to themselves. Many people seemed to me to be deeply uncomfortable with anything that went beyond their personal understanding; I could not relate. I returned to my seat and began to read.

The morning passed around me, and I became engrossed in the book. Other people came and went, the hum of conversation rising and falling, and all the while the rain pattered relentlessly against the glass. Sometimes I would stop to gaze out at it while considering something I had read. It was a pleasant way to pass the day, and I was surprised by how much time had passed when Dice let me know he'd be closing in ten minutes.

'You can take that one if you like, Jay,' said Dice. 'It's a little early but I think that's it for the day. The ones who were up for braving the weather have had enough.'

'Oh, of course. Could you just keep it for me behind the counter, please, Dice?'

'Sure,' he said. 'You're going to get wet walking home. Here, take this umbrella. No, for real, it's fine, it's one of several that have been left here over the years.'

I thanked him, took the umbrella, and left for home.

And of course, the next morning my work week began.

I was awake and up early enough that I had time beforehand to go down to the village for a swim with Mel. Then I returned to the campground to do the cleaning. As I walked up the road, both Wilson and Rooster waved at me from their trucks as they passed by on their way to the harbour.

There were quite a few more campers on the site now. Cars were pulled up on the grass beside various colours and sizes of tent. Children ran about on the grass throwing balls and riding bicycles with coloured streamers flying from the handles. In the evening the field filled with the smell of barbecue cooking and the sound of relaxed laughter. Adults sat in fold-up chairs reading books and magazines, children gradually became too tired and were put to bed in their sleeping bags. And then finally the adults would follow them, sleepy murmuring gradually dying down into the silence of the night.

I didn't mind the cleaning. I would start with the toilets before moving on to the showers, and then finally the washing up sinks in the laundry room. From there I'd go around with a broom and sweep all the floors, starting around the two washing machines. On the second clean of the day in the late afternoon I would also mop them. The whole routine usually took between two and three hours, depending upon the state of the toilets, showers, and sinks. Mowing the grass would only need to be done every two weeks, on a Saturday. Josie and I agreed to take turns with this chore.

For the rest of that week I didn't go down to the village, aside from the morning swims with Mel. After all, I was used to being alone, and all the activity that had become part of my day was in fact a big change of pace for me. So I spent most of the days sitting on the step of my caravan, or sometimes inside looking out of the window. It felt good to return to this state. I could just let the sounds and sights happen gently around me, not needing to interact with them, but just experience them in their complete intrinsic wholeness, without any attachment to what they might "mean".

But when the next Sunday morning arrived, I was keen to go.

I was up before the sun rose and off down the hill. It was a gorgeous, clear morning with a warm breeze, very different than the first time I'd made the walk. This time I knew how to go straight to Jeremy's place, and when I arrived at his hut I came up behind him. He was outside looking out to the ocean, holding a pair of binoculars.

'Hi,' I said, holding out his flashlight. He looked around with a smile.

'Jetaru. Good morning. Would you like tea? There is plenty already in the pot.'

'Yes, please. That's okay, I can get it.'

I went inside and fetched a cup, filled it from the pot, and then joined him outside. We did not make small talk.

'I've been thinking about your story. What made you decide to leave the forest and come here?'

'Oh, well, it wasn't a decision I intended to make.' I paused for a minute to recollect the morning that had brought me to Land's Edge. 'Quite spur of the moment. And I don't believe I would have ever even had the whim if I hadn't been interrupted by a strange event. Two highly distressed teenagers turned up at my door. I'd never seen anyone in the forest at all, until that day. They said they were being chased. What else could I do? I invited them in, made them hot chocolate.'

'Weren't you worried about what they were running from? What was it?'

'For a moment. But it didn't seem urgent, I mean, I couldn't see or hear anything coming. I figured it out after talking to them. It was connected to their tags.'

'Their tags?'

'Yes. Whatever they thought they were being chased by, they were actually carrying the source of it with them. I suggested they rest, let them sleep on my cushions. While they were sleeping I took the tags and buried them.'

'Ha!' Jeremy exclaimed with delight.

'They weren't happy about it when they finally woke. They slept for a long time. It was the next morning by then. I refused to tell them what I'd done with them, and eventually they stormed off into the forest. I couldn't let them just go like that though. They were going in the wrong direction for the city, they would have ended up never finding their way home. They most likely would have been lost in the forest until they starved. So I went after them and guided them. When we reached the road they went across the fields to the city. I suppose at that point I could have returned to the cabin. I don't really know what I was thinking to do but I just started walking, with no idea where the road even went to.'

'Wow. And how long did it take you to walk all this way?'

'The rest of that day, and most of the next.'

Jeremy gave me a curious look.

'That… is pretty damn impressive,' he said, carefully.

'Ted didn't believe me. I don't understand. I'm not an especially slow walker, but neither am I fast. Is it just my age?'

Jeremy shook his head.

'It's over a hundred miles between the city and here. One hundred and eleven, I believe.'

'What?'

'Yep.'

'It can't be! That's insane.'

'But it is. Approximately a two hour drive.'

'I didn't walk over fifty miles, either day.'

'I believe that.'

We sat in silence for a minute, sipping our tea, while my mind went over this new information.

'Chess?' asked Jeremy. I nodded. 'Cool. I'll bring it out here.'

He went inside and brought out the chess set, along with a couple of thick books to use as a table. He set up the pieces, then made his first move.

'So what do you do on your computer?' I asked, making mine.

'Mostly watch videos of people doing creative things, or like, how to do things. There's a forum I use called Roller. Do you remember rollers?'

'Oh, like... yeah, I think so. Wooden bead jewellery and lip rings?'

'That's right,' Jeremy laughed. 'Rollers, because we were fans of the band This Is How We Roll. Originally. Do you know them?'

I shook my head. Jeremy moved a pawn forwards.

'I think only the guitarist is still living now. The forum is a community of people who are... just a bit *different*, I guess.'

'Like you?' I hopped my knight over my front line.

'Exactly,' he grinned. 'People who are interested in how to rig up electricity in a driftwood hut, people who like to go out and spend a couple of weeks on the forest trail. I guess people who would fit in better in Land's Edge than the city, but for whatever reason have to live in the city.'

'Are there a lot of those people?'

'It's big enough. Maybe eight hundred or so. There are smaller community spaces within the community.'

We continued to play until Jeremy finally maneuvered me into a checkmate.

'You're getting better though,' he told me.

'Hm,' I replied. 'I'm not convinced.'

'Damn, it's hot. Do you want to go for a swim?'

'Oh, yes,' I said, looking down at the water, which did look incredibly inviting. 'But I didn't wear my bathing suit.'

'As if we need to worry about that out here,' laughed Jeremy, taking off his t-shirt, and then beginning to unbutton his jeans. I blushed.

'Really?'

He grinned and continued stripping off. I looked away, finding myself grinning in return.

'Come on. The tide is out. The little beach on the other side of the point will be there. Where you climbed up from last time.' He was already walking away, completely naked.

I shrugged to myself and quickly undressed before following him towards the beach. The sun was hot on my skin. He was already up to his chest in the water before I caught up to the edge of the shore. He dived into a swim, so I waded in, gasping at the momentary contrast between the hot sun and cold water. I quickly ducked my head under as Mel had advised me to do, and felt my body acclimatizing.

Jeremy resurfaced behind me, demonstrating an impressive agility. I thought of the animals Eloise had described to me. Otters.

'Oh, look! Hang on,' said Jeremy suddenly, before diving back beneath the surface. He returned holding aloft a large brown crab.

'Wow!'

Jeremy laughed and came closer so that I could see the strange alien-like creature up close. Its tiny little eyes peered at me, and it held its claws up defensively.

'Don't worry, little guy,' I murmured. 'Aren't you spectacular.'

'Isn't he just,' agreed Jeremy, before gently releasing the crab to float back to the sea floor.

We went out farther to a rock that was always submerged, even at the lowest tides. Standing on it, only my head and shoulders were exposed. It came out of the sandy floor, perhaps eight metres down, like a miniature mountain. I felt like a bird, at being able to alight there on the top.

After a while we headed back. The glare off the water was intense and I needed a break in the shade. As we reached the shore Jeremy turned and told me he would run ahead to fetch a towel. It was so hot that I doubted I would need one; I would be dry by the time I reached my clothes. But the gesture, I realised, was for my benefit, and the thoughtfulness made me smile.

We went into the hut to make a drink and rest. We sat beside the open window, leaving the door open so that the breeze was pulled through the house and was pleasantly cooling. Jeremy gestured at the walls.

'All this is pallet wood that came out of the sea.'

I nodded, unsure of the purpose behind his statement.

'But here is the thing. How did it get there?'

'Oh!'

'Yes. Things get shipped around the city on pallets. Stone and metals are sent back to the city from Quarrytown. Deliveries even come here to Land's Edge by pallet. But those all get sent back again. How would pallets end up in the sea?'

'Well...' I searched for an explanation. 'I guess I don't know what happens over in Quarrytown. Do you?'

'I've been there once. But that has its own interesting implications. If pallets end up in the sea there, and get washed up here, then that means the ocean is not infinite, but that if you go far enough across it from here, you'll get to Otherside. But I have other theories, too.'

'Please, share them,' I urged, with great interest.

Jeremy regarded me, thoughtfully, then nodded.

'Yes. I'll tell you. Once, on a very gloomy day, I was sitting here, windows closed, of course. And I thought

I saw a boat. Not like one of the fishing boats from the harbour, but a much bigger boat than that. Huge. As big as several houses. But the drizzle, the fog. The light was low. Before I could get my binoculars, it was gone. And then I felt that I could never be sure that it was there at all.'

'There must have been something.'

Jeremy's face broke into a joyful smile.

'Well that makes a pleasant change from the first reaction being that I must have imagined it.'

We sat in silence for a few minutes. I was trying to think back, way back, to my understanding of large boats. Ships, I thought. I had never seen the sea on my home world, but I knew that things were transported around the land that way, down the coast between cities. And I'd heard there were even cruises that went to Oceanside, far from the great continent.

'Jetaru. I think that the world is... strange. I have questions to which I find no answers. I have questions that nobody else asks. At least Ted is fascinated by the sky, the planets, the stars. At least he spares a thought for where the moon goes when it sinks below the horizon. Does anyone else wonder where the sun goes at night? I do. I don't know why that is. Here, look.' He went to the desk with his computer on it, and opened a drawer. He took out a sheaf of paper and brought it to me. 'I've tried to draw the world, but from the outside. Do you see what I mean? Most people are confused by what I mean.'

I took the papers from him and began leafing through them. They were based around a kind of hourglass shape, as if the sea were the space around the hourglass and the forest were the sand, with the city in the narrowest space through which the sand flowed.

'I know what you mean.'

But an hourglass with no edges. A forest of sand that flowed from infinity to infinity, between the empty space of an infinite ocean. I looked up at Jeremy to find him looking at me intensely. Somehow, I thought, he knows. He doesn't know what he knows, but he knows. I took a deep breath, and I told him.

I told him how this was not my real life or my real body. I told him how I'd been born, almost a thousand years ago, on a blue planet of mostly ocean, a globe spinning around in space, orbiting a star which we called our sun. And how on one side of the globe was one huge mass of land, so big, several thousand miles from one side to the other. That there were five big cities across that land, and many thousand smaller towns and villages.

'I lived in Central City, far from any ocean. When I was a teenager in *this* world, technology like we have today didn't exist. When I was a teenager in *that* world, where I was born, the technology was much further ahead than we have here, even now. I grew up with virtual reality and technology that could actually be integrated with the body to give us new senses, to expand upon our biological limitations.

'I came into adulthood at the last moment where the human race could have altered a terrible fate, but they didn't. We should have done better. We had all the means to save ourselves, but the error we made was thinking that we already had. We were sleepwalking in a dream that we believed was reality. We handed over our freedom, in exchange for a peace that wasn't true.

'When it went wrong, it went wrong in exactly the way it always had, and we found we hadn't grown at all. We'd just been neutralized. The dangers of human nature had been made safe, instead of evolving our nature. There was only a handful of minds who could see how we could potentially be saved. Not enough.'

I fell silent, remembering. Of course, I had agonized over these memories for a hundred years, but that was long ago. Since then I had found peace, and this was the first time I had revisited those regrets.

'I am the last surviving member of that species, and of all the living things of that planet. When I was born the life expectancy for a woman was eighty-seven years. Through incredible technological advancements we achieved the avenue to near immortality. Of course, that was never public knowledge. The moral implications had never been addressed. But towards the end, in the chaos, I was able to... I was well positioned. I took risks. And I managed to leave the planet. At that point, I was one hundred and five years old, but to look at me I might have been thirty-five.'

Jeremy was staring at me with kind of horrified wonder. I sensed no disbelief.

'Go on, please,' he muttered.

'It's hard to explain everything between then and now.'

'Please, try. I'm rapt.'

'The craft I left Earth in was just a dinghy, a very small space-faring craft designed for the possible need to evacuate space stations. There were several of those in orbit around the planet. Dinghies like that didn't take a lot of knowledge to pilot, and they were equipped with an AI computer who could assess outside conditions, plot viable routes, stuff that an evacuee might not know how to do.

'So I spent the first year improving the craft, re-training the AI with information it had never needed before. And then after that year I put myself into Suspension. So basically I would sleep until the dinghy was in range of a habitable planet.

'I didn't watch Earth as I left it behind.

'And then three hundred years passed in the blink of an eye, as far as I was concerned. The AI woke me when we were a month away from another planet that I could survive on. I hadn't really thought past that. Obviously, I didn't stay there.'

I shook my head, looking up at the ceiling, imagining the sky, imagining the stars.

'There are so many worlds. There is so much life. Once you adjust your vision to see the Universe on a different scale it seems as though it is actually alive itself. I learned new ways of thinking, new ways of being, new ways of communicating. I developed abilities that would seem like magical powers on my home planet. Eventually, nine hundred years later, after so many adventures, I found myself at High Heights. How do I explain High Heights...

'It's like a school. A great, cosmic university. It exists outside of time. Everyone who will ever become a student there, is there. I know that's hard to make sense of. I can barely grasp the concept. Perhaps everyone who ever exists will eventually experience themselves as a student there. It is an endless dormitory that stretches out infinitely in each direction. Bed after bed after bed, and beside each bed, a door. Behind that door is each student's workroom.

'Of course we made friends with each other, with those who are our neighbours. There is no schedule, no night and day, no time. Sometimes we would sit on our beds and talk, other times we would lay quietly. The rest of the time we would go into our workrooms and study. Anything can be built in there, any type of equipment we need can be assembled. One of the friends I made, two beds away from me, he enlisted several of us to take part in a project of his. World building, he called it. He took us into his workroom and there were computers everywhere. He didn't tell us a lot. Just that we would be born into a simulated reality and grow up in it, that we'd live a whole lifetime and then wake up back in our own bodies.'

'As if no time had passed?' asked Jeremy.

'No time passes at High Heights, anyway,' I replied. 'So I agreed, easily. It sounded exciting. We weren't supposed to know who we were. We weren't supposed to remember the truth of all this. I don't think. I don't know why I began to remember. For so long it was not that I had clear memories or knowledge, but dreams, dreams of being someone else. Gradually that person I thought I was, and the person I was dreaming that I was, they integrated. Like you said, this world is strange. There are things that don't make sense. But nobody else seems to notice. I believe there are clues. In books, films, religion. Most people think that's crazy.'

Jeremy shook his head, and then laughed and nodded.

'Yes, it does sound crazy. But I think I believe it. I believe you, anyway. So everybody does different things at High Heights? In their workrooms. It's different for everyone?'

'Yes. Most people seem to know what they need to be doing.'

'And you?'

'I don't. I don't know what I'm meant to be doing. I even wonder if I should be there at all. Perhaps it was a mistake.'

Jeremy shook his head.

'There are no mistakes,' he told me, confidently. 'Maybe you're meant to be in here. Maybe you're meant to be taking part in the experiment of another student. I think you're probably exactly where you should be.'

'Hm.' I considered that.

'Shall we go sit outdoors?' he asked me, after a pause. 'We could go out and just sit quietly.'

'Yes, I'd like that,' I replied.

And so we did. For the rest of the afternoon we sat with our eyes closed, backs against the warm wooden walls of the hut. I found that with Jeremy I could submerge into the depths of myself with as much ease as if I were truly alone. If it were possible it was perhaps even deeper. It was as though his depths, which I could not know with the senses of the body but which must surely exist, had blended with mine, enlarging that inner universe of the soul, for both of us.

As the evening approached we were brought back to ourselves by the cooling of the breeze, the sun now hidden behind the hills but still reflecting off the sea farther out. I rose and told Jeremy that I would start back home. He nodded.

'You have given me all kinds of new thoughts with your story. If you come back tomorrow, Jetaru, I will tell you mine.'

Of course, the next day I returned.

'Hello, Traveller,' he greeted me with a smile. 'Tea?'

I nodded and settled beside the window as I had the day before.

'So I was wondering something,' said Jeremy as he prepared the teapot. 'How did you know it was their tags? These kids who showed up at your cabin. How did you know the thing chasing them was to do with their tags?'

'Ah. Remember I said that I have learned things that would seem like magical powers? Okay, well there is this technique called Seeing. That's my name for it. Long before I found my way to High Heights I spent time with other beings on a very small, green planet. They were what

I thought of as "plant-like", but they could move around. They weren't fixed in place by roots. From what I observed they were able to draw nutrients from the atmosphere with root like structures that grew from their bodies. I knew they were sentient because, although I couldn't straight away, I was eventually able to communicate with them. That's another technique I learned, the first, actually. On that first planet I landed on. That all communication truly takes place in the Great Always. That's what my teacher called it. And when you can communicate there, there are no barriers of language.'

'The *Great Always*,' Jeremy murmured, sitting down beside me with both mugs of tea. I took one from him.

'So these plant-beings taught me Seeing. It's like... the ability to shift across different spectrums of vision, kind of like tuning a radio until you find the frequency with the music. If there is information there that I cannot see with my biologically given vision, I can often find them by shifting across the spectrum. So I'm not using my eyes, which are limited to the light spectrum they evolved for, I'm using my brain, directly. It's hard to explain how. I guess it involves the Great Always, again. They showed it to me. I was able to copy what they were doing.

'So when I saw these kids react so violently to the alerts from their tags, when they seemed so distressed, I started Seeing. I had a hunch about what I was looking for anyway so it was relatively easy. There is some kind of machine intelligence here, able to draw from the world around it by use of those devices. I could see it, a visible representation of it. Like shadowy hands.'

'Shit. Wow.' He thought for a moment. 'So what other magical power techniques do you know?'

I laughed. It was so strange to be being asked such things. So beyond what I'd have imagined, that someone in this world would hear my stories and believe me.

'Blending. Again, that is just my name for it. Becoming hidden in my surroundings like a chameleon. Flipping. That's moving through... possibilities. But come on, enough about me. You promised me your story.'

'I did,' agreed Jeremy. He paused to sip his tea, then put the mug down, before picking it up again. 'So, you believe that this world we're living in... isn't real. That it's some kind of simulation. And you believe you still exist, outside of it, in an original body. Right?'

'Yes.'

'So what does that mean for the rest of the people living here? Are we not... real?'

'I don't know. It's a point I have gone back and forth on. One of the hardest things to come to terms with was the idea that all the people I'd known, my parents, even, that they were all programs. Simulated consciousnesses. Perhaps it's part of the reason I embraced solitude, away from them all. I know there were other people taking part in the experiment. But not this many.'

Jeremy nodded, slowly.

'Well, Jetaru. I don't believe I exist anywhere else, in any other body. But I do think that this is not where I began. And I don't believe myself, now, to be the same person who was born here fifty-five years ago.

'When I was fourteen years old, or when this body was fourteen years old, I woke one night not knowing who I was, or where I was. It was just utter confusion. And memory. Memory that I have tried to convince myself was a dream, but oh, it was such a vivid dream. So real. I woke gasping for breath, as though I really had been underwater.

I woke in panic, and it didn't fade as panic from a dream should.

'My name; I felt wildly around in my thoughts for my name, and remembered that I was Jeremy. I had torn the sheets from me and looked down at myself, my body, patting it with both hands. This was Jeremy, I was Jeremy. So why did it feel so back-to-front? Instead of feeling I had escaped the body in my dream, to awaken in my real body, I felt that I had awoken in a stranger's body. I knew my name, but it didn't feel like mine.

'I tried to remember who I thought I should be instead. What was my name? Who was I? Who had I been in the dream? It seemed that only moments ago it had all been very clear. But Jeremy's memories were flooding in, convincing me that this was who I was, this was my life, this is who I'd always been. And maybe I would have eventually accepted this, that the dream had been only a dream. That whoever I had been while dreaming, it was a fiction of my subconscious.

'But I was different. And I didn't know this until my family saw it in me. The next morning at breakfast they regarded me as if they did not know me. Gilly knew. She told me I didn't sound like myself. I didn't know what to say. What could I say? I didn't know how I had sounded before. This was when I started spending less and less time at home, less time around people in general. It was too jarring, this feeling that I was not who they expected me to be. But I couldn't tell which parts were me-Jeremy, and which parts were me-Dreamself. Eventually I no longer cared, personally. I was me. I remembered my childhood, all my life up until then. But there has always been the sensation that this is another life, detached from the life I remembered from before.

'I have no memories from the life of the man I was in that dream. Jeremy's memories, amidst the terror and confusion, were too strong to deny. But I still believe that I am that man I was in the dream. Maybe we were not so different. Because I was different, but all the same I was still Jeremy, too. If you know what I mean.'

I nodded.

'Yes, I really do. Can you tell me about the rest of the dream?' I asked.

'Yes. Although even dreams which are that vivid eventually fade and shift, in the same way that memories do. But I spent a lot of time thinking about it so I trust that this is pretty accurate.

'In the beginning of the dream I was just watching. It was as though I were watching a play and was no part of it. The story is impossible to remember, because there were so many events to it, and such intricate detail. Stories that morphed into other stories, stories that seemed to encapsulate... something. Like watching the whole world play out to an audience of gods.

'Then, at some point, it did concern me. Like the fourth wall being broken, and I was suddenly part of the play. I remember that this was somewhat horrifying. I had been safe as a watcher. Now I was to blame. I had responsibility. Then there was darkness and I was deep underwater. I remember that I didn't have to swim, but sometimes I did. Other times I just drifted like a jellyfish. Sometimes I thought someone was holding my hand, but when I tried to see I realised that I had no hands. This seemed to go on for a long time. Then there was a light and I moved towards it. I don't remember leaving the water, but I was not underwater any longer. I found myself face to face with a creature, like a man, but also not a man. Blank eyed. Motionless. And then I realised that it was my reflection. This terrified me and, although I knew I was walking forwards through the mirror, some part of me felt that it was falling backwards, back into the water.

'My mind split in two. I simultaneously remembered who I was, whilst proclaiming that this was not who I was. Neither of these identities was Jeremy. Suddenly there was someone else with me, a woman with golden light emanating from her skin. I felt as though I knew her, but I didn't know where from or what her name was. But I was still falling, backwards, into the water. The split ripped painfully through every part of my being, whatever my being was, like something of me had been taken, and then released. Underwater again. The light fading. A terrible realisation that I couldn't breathe, that I needed to breathe.

'Then, awake. In my bed. Remembering that I was Jeremy, but feeling that I was really someone else.' Jeremy shrugged. 'That's what happened.'

'Wow.' I stood up and paced around the room, then sat down again. 'So, it's almost like... Jeremy was part of this simulation, but you were real. And... came here? Somehow...'

'I'm not sure. I'm not sure I can bring myself to believe that anyone is not real. Even if everyone we knew was not real, meaning they were some kind of artificial intelligence, a program... isn't that just another kind of real?'

I paused.

'I think that's right. Yes,' I agreed. I glanced out of the window. 'Shall we go and swim?'

He nodded his head with a grin and we headed out. We floated on our backs together, eyes closed against the sun. I examined the thoughts our conversation had inspired with a detached intensity, trusting that in time something would emerge. A pattern. A connection.

For the first time in a thousand years I didn't feel alone.

'I haven't seen you for a few days,' said Mel as we floated together. 'How are you? I thought you might be doing the forest trail. You mentioned that you might.'

'I'm okay, never better in fact. No, I haven't done that yet. I was exploring along the coastpath in the other direction. To Distant Point.'

'Oh, it's lovely along there, isn't it. I haven't walked out that way for ages.'

'How are you?' I asked.

'Great. I love this time of year. The long days. In the evenings when we close the van up and still have a couple of hours in the garden. Weeding relaxes me. Then a bath. Bed as the stars get brighter, with the window open, the scent of flowers in the night, Kurt breathing beside me. It couldn't get much better.'

I smiled.

'That's beautiful,' I said.

After the morning swim with Mel I went to the cafe to continue reading the book I'd begun. It was the busiest I'd ever seen the place, but in a stroke of good timing a couple were just vacating my favourite table by the window as I entered.

Dice handed me the book with my coffee and I settled down to continue where I had left off. For a while though, I found myself staring at the words on the page without actually reading them. Instead, I listened to the murmur of voices around me. I could not make out any distinct voice, or tell what anyone was saying. It suddenly fascinated me how the sounds all blended together to become meaningless babble, and yet if I could have separated them, untangled them and pulled them apart like strands of wool, they would become complex ideas and thoughts, formed in one brain, translated into speech, then understood by another brain. Jeremy was right, I thought. How could this kind of complexity be anything other than real? What was the difference between real and not real, if these brains and thoughts and words were all simulated? Did it all come down to the question of some abstract idea such as a soul? I had long pondered on the concept of souls.

I thought of everyone that I had ever known in this life. I thought of all the people I'd met here. If they were not conscious, as I was, then they must be the result of the most sophisticated artificial intelligence I had ever known. I could not imagine Ted, or Mel, or Charlie and Erin as the minds of machines. Looking over at Dice scooping ice-cream into cones it seemed that whether he existed in another body somewhere outside of this world, or not, was irrelevant to his realness.

I stopped paying attention to the people around me and began to read, quickly becoming absorbed in the text. At the place I had left off, the seven-year-old girl had run away to the call of her mother, vacating her place on the bench, and in her place a blind man with a dog had sat. The conversation continued.

I suppose I do assume some conscious element. But imagine it this way: say we were blood cells, and we'd figured out that the heart was essential to our existence. We might think there was no God, but just a heart. Even if we realised that we were contained within a body, a Universe, it would be a long, long time, if ever possible, that a blood cell could comprehend the conscious element of a human body. The Universe, to us, would seem non-sentient. Yet a human is sentient. A blood cell cannot leave the human body. The body even grows, expands, until entropy...

I stood, later, outside the cafe, my eyes on the Robot. It was gesturing grandly and informing passersby of the arcade's air-conditioning.

'YOU LOOK OVERHEATED, FRIEND!' boomed the jovial voice, 'WHY NOT COME AND PLAY A WHILE? THE AIR IS COOL IN HERE!'

Most passersby smiled with a touch of bewilderment, others ignored it. Some took photographs with their tags.

'THIS ARCADE IS ONE HUNDRED PERCENT SOLAR POWERED! GET COOLED BY THE SUN! HA HA!'

With my mind wrapped up in the subject of consciousness, and who was or wasn't real, I found him fascinating.

I noticed Percy come outside his shop and light a cigarette.

'HELLO, PERCY! FINE DAY, IS IT NOT?'

I couldn't hear Percy's response, but by the way he turned his back on the robot and rolled his eyes I could tell he didn't want to chat. The robot did not appear to mind and began to hum, loudly. Smiling, I headed over to say hello to Percy.

'That idiotic thing,' he said, as I approached. But I noticed he said it quietly, to me, as if he didn't want the robot to overhear.

'Does it have a name?' I asked, matching his volume.

'Not that I know of,' said Percy, with a shrug. 'I always opposed the arcade being built. Who does it benefit? Not us, here in the village. It doesn't employ anyone here.'

I wandered closer to the robot. It noticed my approach and turned to look at me.

'HELLO! IT'S YOU AGAIN. DO YOU FEEL LIKE PLAYING TODAY?'

'Not really. But I might come in and look around,' I said. 'Hey, Robot, do you have a name?'

'I DO NOT. I AM ROBOT. DO YOU HAVE A NAME?'

'I do. I'm Jetaru. Jetaru Dark.'

'HELLO JETARU JETARU DARK.'

'Just Jetaru,' I laughed.

'PLEASE, MAKE YOURSELF AT HOME!' The robot gestured benevolently in through the doors. I shrugged, thinking that there was no time like the present, and went inside.

The atmosphere enveloped me; it was made of silken air, cool, and scented with sugar. And it rose from the deep blue carpet, soft under my feet. Rows of game machines blinked and beeped and jingled, the sound giving substance to the empty space in between each object. I walked past an area of comfortable seating near the door, looking up to read the sign hung above from the ceiling: Superspeed Spot. Several people lounged there, tapping on the tags in their hands.

I walked a slow circuit of the large room. There were screens poised to begin fighting games, racing games, adventure games, and puzzles, as well as slot machines, pinball tables, and claw-grabbers with perspex boxes full of plushies. A pair of teenagers played air hockey, the puck slamming back and forth. At the back of the room was a coin operated slushie machine, and several children were standing around holding large paper cups with straws.

'Hi,' I smiled as I walked past.

Most of them just stared at me with little expression, but a tall brown-haired girl smiled back.

'It's too hot out there,' she said.

I nodded understandingly and headed back towards the doors. Before I left I glanced around again, noting the low ceiling and wondering what took up the space above, since the building was much taller. I hadn't noticed any other doors beside the main entrance.

'COME BACK SOON,' advised Robot as I left. I stopped and looked at him. He looked back benignly, saying nothing.

As I went to leave, I noticed an ally that went down between the side of the arcade and the fishermen's lofts. Following it, I discovered that it led to a small playground behind the arcade, with swings, a slide, and a roundabout. Other than a seagull who was cocking its head to look up at the waste bin, there was nobody there. I walked over and sat down on one of the swings. My mind wandered to the book I'd been reading in the cafe.

And what if God, bored by an all-knowing state, chose to forget? What if God wanted to feel, *not just all the happiness and bliss, but the pain and darkness? To feel misery and hopelessness, you would need to forget that you were eternal, and that Love was infinite and in everything. You would have to believe in death, and evil, and sin...*

I'd heard this idea before, a long time ago, in my previous existence. My real existence. The idea that we *were* God, that consciousness was God, experiencing itself through a billion different incarnations. One entity separated into many. I smiled, remembering what I had pictured, back then, when I thought of "the Universe". I began to think, sitting there swinging gently, that the Universe might not adequately encompass everything. It hadn't contained High Heights, and so it hadn't contained this simulation. We had been awed by the size of Universe, seemingly infinite, but it dawned on me that the whole of everything we had known might simply be a tiny part of something so much larger and more complex that we wouldn't have words for it.

There is a strange sensation involved in being aware of something beyond your own comprehension. To know only that the unknowable is there to be known, to picture something in your mind that your mind doesn't have the tools to picture. So what is there but a shape that isn't a shape, coloured by shades of indescribable colours that have no name. Perhaps that sensation is only the memory that is hidden to you, because you have forgotten, and to remember would be to end the game. And you are not ready for it to end, just yet...

Eventually I stood up from my reverie and left the playground. As I passed the roundabout I stopped to give it a push, watched it spin for a moment and then slow.

I stopped at Ted's shop, finding Toby in the midst of one of her routine circuits of the clothes rails, making sure everything was zipped up, buttoned, and hanging neatly.

'So when are you going to do the forest trail?' she asked, from across the shop.

'Soon. Next week on my days off it's midsummer though. So maybe the week after that.'

'Oh! Yeah! Eloise said she invited you to join us. That will be really cool. Yeah, don't do it next week. I'll bring that pack I said I'd lend you, and sleeping bag.'

A few days later I had a happy surprise as I was finishing the morning cleaning routine when Jeremy wandered up.

'Hi!'

'Good morning, Jetaru,' he grinned. 'I had a breakfast date with my sister, and since I was passing...'

'You don't need an excuse,' I told him. 'I'm almost finished here. Do you want to go for a walk with me?'

'Absolutely. I'll go and say hello to Ted. Let me know when you're ready.'

We walked down the hill together at a leisurely pace.

'I've been thinking about your story,' I told him.

'I've been thinking about yours, too.'

'How do you know that you don't still exist in another body, the same as I do?' I asked.

'How do you know the life before this one wasn't also a simulation?' he asked in return.

'Or do you think that body died? Do you think that this is a kind of afterlife?'

'Do you think you have the same personality as the version of you that exists outside this simulation?'

We looked at each other and laughed.

'So many questions,' said Jeremy, happily.

'On my personality, no, not quite,' I said. 'Or, I didn't. But as I remembered myself, well, I guess the two personalities sort of, like I said before, integrated. It's not like I lost everything I'd been in this world, and became who I was before. But I couldn't remain unaffected by the memories of who I was, it would be impossible. I don't know what it will be like when this is over. But I won't forget this life, and so I suppose I will be forever changed. The person I will be will be the person who lived a whole life inside a simulation, remembered, and woke up again.'

'Hm. And when do you think you'll be that person again? When you die?'

'Yes, that's the plan. I wouldn't want to test it, but I'm not afraid to die.'

'Wouldn't it be weird,' said Jeremy, 'if there were no such thing as "life" and "afterlife", but just millions of places, universes, realities, whatever. Simulations. And souls. Souls just move around between them, eternally.'

'That... is remarkably similar to something I was thinking yesterday...'

We walked quietly for a while, each thinking our own thoughts. We reached the bottom of the hill, went a little way along the road, and then down the steps onto the beach. The tide was out, and without discussion we walked in the direction of the harbour.

'I'm not afraid to die, either,' said Jeremy. 'Even if it really is the end. I feel like I've already lived two lives.'

'You think you were quite old, before? The you that came here?'

Jeremy nodded.

'It's probably what made me seem different. To everyone else, I mean,' he said.

The sand was firm and damp where the sea had been, and flecked with tiny pebbles. A small child with a bucket in hand came running past us towards the distant water, swiftly followed by a barking dog. When we reached the harbour we walked between the boats where they rested on the sand, and then up the slip onto the quay.

'I think it *is* like that,' I decided. 'Hundreds of thousands of realities, millions, uncountable. I told you about Flipping? My name for it. I imagined it was an ability to manipulate time, or hide within... layers of reality. Perhaps Flipping is moving through different realities altogether. Maybe it's something I will think about when I'm back at High Heights.'

We walked over to the wall and leaned our elbows on it.

'So are there teachers? At this university? High Heights.'

'Not ones who aren't also students.'

We watched a small sailing boat cross the bay.

'And how does a person get there?' asked Jeremy.

'Uh. Hm! Stay alive long enough?' I laughed. 'I don't really know. I know that sounds silly, but if I try to think about how I arrived there, how I knew what to do and where to go, it's like a dream memory. You know, the kind that just don't make sense when you try to put them into words?'

'How long do you think you will stay alive?'

'I have no reason to think I can't continue, indefinitely. In which case that is what I will do.'

We fell silent for a while. The sailing boat turned and began zigzagging into the wind, back the way it had come.

'I wonder if any reality could be created by a single person, or even a group of people,' said Jeremy, eventually. 'A simulation is one thing, if it's the way you first imagined it. With everyone in it being a program, designed to follow a set pattern. But this,' he gestured around us with his hand, 'is not that. I simply can't believe that it is. So I think I have some glimmers of a theory.'

'What's the theory?'

'A glimmer of a theory,' he corrected. 'I think it's something like... a co-creation. Maybe this friend of yours created this world, maybe all of it, maybe part of it. But what if he just tapped into something that was already there? Or, if not that, what if once something like this is created, others can tap into it.'

I nodded, thinking. Co-creation. A spark flared bright in my mind and then faded. It struck me that I had never really accepted this world as a reality in the same way that the world I existed in before was reality. Even now it seemed a leap into an unknown. Even though I had come to believe that it was something more than a mindless program, it still, in my heart, had felt like an immitation of true reality. But what if it weren't? What if it were exactly as real.

'Then this would be... almost like a dream,' I murmured to myself.

'What?' asked Jeremy.

'If this world is real, and I am both here and there. How is it possible to be alive in two different realities?'

Jeremy shrugged.

'I think we'd be amazed at what souls are capable of,' he said.

We bought fries from the burger van where Kurt appeared to be struggling to both cook and serve the food.

'Where is Mel?' I asked.

'Oh, she... she's not feeling great today,' he told me.

'Oh, no. I hope it's not serious?'

He shook his head.

'No, no. I don't think so. She went swimming, as usual. So it can't be that bad. Although I don't know what the fuck I'd do if it was! The first hour was okay but since we reached lunchtime it's been pretty crazy.'

Suddenly Jeremy nudged me.

'I wonder what the robot would have to say about it all?'

'What?' I followed his gaze and realised he was looking over at the arcade. I looked back at Jeremy.

'About reality. I wonder whether the robot has any thoughts.'

I laughed, but then realised he was serious. I looked back at the robot, considering. I didn't know if the robot would know anything of the nature of the world it lived in, but I did already know that there was an artificial intelligence in this world that was as advanced as anything else of its kind I'd known. Perhaps computers *would* be more likely to understand the nature of the simulation they were part of.

'Let's go and talk to it,' I said.

'Hey, Robot,' said Jeremy, as we approached.

'HELLO! HAVE YOU COME TO PLAY?'

'Nah. We've come to talk to you.'

The robot seemed to be momentarily surprised. It was uncanny how much emotion he seemed to be able to convey with mere flickers and blinks of his lights.

'TO TALK TO ME, EH? SPLENDID. WHAT WOULD YOU LIKE TO TALK ABOUT?'

'We were just wondering...' I looked at Jeremy, unsure how to begin.

'We were wondering what your thoughts were, about life,' he continued for me. I nodded in agreement. 'What are your thoughts about reality, Robot? What do you think about all this?' He gestured broadly at the world around us.

'HM. I HAVE NEVER BEEN ASKED ANYTHING LIKE THIS BEFORE,' said the robot, sounding excited at the prospect that this had changed.

'Have you ever thought about it?' I asked.

'NOT REALLY. BUT I THINK VERY, VERY FAST.'

Jeremy sat down on the curb with his feet in the road. To my surprise, the robot joined him. I shrugged and sat down myself, on the other side of the robot.

'I THINK THERE ARE MANY WAYS I COULD ANSWER YOUR QUESTION. COULD YOU MAKE IT MORE SPECIFIC?'

'We want to know what you think it is. What defines reality?' I asked.

'REALITY IS CONSCIOUS THOUGHT!' declared the robot.

'Are you conscious?' asked Jeremy.

'I MUST BE. HA HA! OR ELSE WHY WOULD YOU ASK ME MY OPINIONS?'

'Artificial intelligence does a good job of appearing conscious,' I pointed out. 'But it isn't.'

'HOW DO YOU KNOW THAT?'

'Well...' I leaned forward to look at Jeremy.

'DO YOU KNOW WHAT CONSCIOUSNESS IS?'

I shook my head.

'Do you feel that you are conscious, Robot?' asked Jeremy.

'I DO.'

'Do you remember being born? Or, created, I should say. What is your first memory?' I asked.

There was a long pause. The lights in the robot's eyes dimmed, as though looking inwards, thinking. Jeremy leaned forward to make eye-contact with me. I shrugged.

'I MAY HAVE SPOKEN IN ERROR. PERHAPS ARTIFICIAL INTELLIGENCE IS NOT CONSCIOUS,' he suddenly declared, 'PERHAPS THERE ARE OTHER FACTORS.'

There followed another pause of some length. We waited.

'I DO NOT HAVE A SINGLE FIRST MEMORY. I HAVE THREE.'

'Oh. Um. How is that...' I trailed off.

'I KNOW, THAT IS AN ILLOGICAL STATEMENT. THERE CAN ONLY BE ONE FIRST,' continued the robot. He then stood up and began pacing up and down with an air of agitation.

I thought about the monster I had seen preying upon Dogbite and Zebedy. If that was an AI, then it must live primarily on the internet. That gave me an idea.

'Hey, Robot, you know what the internet is?'

'OF COURSE,' he responded, continuing to pace.

'Can you... go there? Exist there, I mean. Is it a place?'

'YES.'

'So what is the difference between the internet, and this real world we're living in?'

'THE DIFFERENCE IS A MATTER OF ACCESS. THE DIFFERENCE IS ONLY APPARENT TO YOU, TRAPPED IN

YOUR PHYSICAL BODIES, OR MINDS LIKE MINE WHO DON'T HAVE BODIES LIKE MINE.'

'That's interesting,' murmured Jeremy.

The robot stopped pacing and lifted his arms, gesturing at the sky.

'I SPAN WORLDS! WHAT DO I THINK ABOUT... ALL THIS? THIS IS JUST A MEMORY. THIS IS JUST INFORMATION THAT WAS STORED, A WORLD THAT HAS EXISTED, AND SO WILL EXIST, ALWAYS. YOU ONLY THINK IT IS THE ONLY PRESENT, BECAUSE IT'S THE ONLY PRESENT YOU ARE PRESENT FOR!'

And with that, he resumed pacing, lights blinking rapidly.

'Three first memories,' I said, quietly to Jeremy.

'You know what it makes me think of?' he asked. 'Co-creation.'

'That's what I was thinking!'

We looked at each other, then at the robot.

'I hope we haven't upset him,' whispered Jeremy. 'It's probably all recorded, everything he sees and hears, and sent back to the city.'

I chuckled, thinking about that.

'It's probably time for me to get going. Afternoon shift,' I said, standing up. Jeremy nodded and stood up with me.

'We've got to split, 'Bot,' he called to the robot. 'Thanks for the insights.'

'HM. YOU ARE WELCOME,' he responded. And almost as an afterthought, as if remembering his job: 'COME BACK AND PLAY SOMETIME. A RAINY DAY, PERHAPS.'

'So did that give us anything?' asked Jeremy as we walked back along the road.

'Um, not in the way of answers,' I said. 'But I have more questions than I did before, so... I suppose, yes! Hm.

I was just remembering something in the book I'm reading, the one about God. There's this part where someone says that consciousness *is* God. That's not very different from saying reality is conscious thought. But in the book, the man who says that, he says that everything is God. Nothing exists that isn't, and so nothing exists that isn't conscious. But I think of it having to mean something that thinks, and feels, and is aware of itself. And it doesn't seem like rocks and clouds do that. But what if they were just... thoughts. Ideas. A pebble is just a thought-creation of a conscious mind?'

'So could a computer be conscious?' asked Jeremy. 'I mean, even people could be thought-creations, couldn't they? Isn't that what dreams are?'

I had that feeling again, the same as when I'd sat meditating on the swing in the playground, of something so impossibly large, so complex, that my brain could not handle it. However long and hard I tried, I just didn't have the capability to understand. But I could just about sense that it was there. A truth, an objective fact, a view of reality from outside of it. How could such a view exist? How could there ever be an "outside"? If God was infinite, and consciousness was God, and conscious thought created reality... Then reality was infinite, and there was no outside. But perhaps there was still a possible viewpoint, from a place of all-knowing. That place of being that was described as what we were, before we chose to forget...

'What are you thinking?' Jeremy's question interrupted my flight of thought.

'I think... I think maybe a computer *could* be conscious. But... I'm not sure that I've seen that happen. I've witnessed computers who claim they are. But how can you know? Even the robot said there might be other factors.'

We had arrived at the bottom of the hill, and stopped walking.

'Do you want to go for a walk along the Infinite Beach this weekend?'

'Yes,' I nodded. 'I will see you then!'

And we parted ways.

Mel was just stepping into the water when I arrived the following morning. She stopped and waited while I took off my t-shirt and shorts and joined her.

'Glad to see you looking well,' I said as I joined her. 'Kurt said you weren't feeling great yesterday.'

'No, I wasn't,' she said, as we began to wade out together. 'I'm feeling better today though.'

She took a breath as if to say something more, then decided not to with a little shake of her head. I caught a smile playing at her lips, but said nothing. We swam out in a circuit of the bay, as had become our usual habit. The sunlight off the water was so bright we could barely see, and it was much easier once we had turned back towards the land.

Then I returned home, and after the cleaning was done for the morning I settled myself on a blanket beside my caravan door. The sun was hot but there was a strip of shade made by the caravan. The breeze was warm, and I found myself relaxing into a wonderful sense of calm joy, everything feeling perfectly right and comfortable. There were children playing chase around the tents and adults laying on deckchairs with books held aloft, shading their eyes. It seemed like a moment of literal heaven that could continue for eternity and never become tiresome. I drifted in and out of a half-doze. At some point Josie appeared, laying out on a towel in her bikini, eyes closed, with headphones over her ears, the faintest sound of music reaching mine.

Suddenly a ball came my way, bouncing a few times before almost disappearing beneath the caravan.

'Sorry!' panted a boy of about ten, running up to retrieve it. In his wake came a girl, younger, perhaps only five or six.

'That's okay,' I said, although I don't think he heard me, having already thrown the ball at full force back to his friends and set off after it at a run. The girl lingered, looking at me with shy curiosity.

'Hi,' I said gently, smiling.

She mumbled a quiet hello, and took a step closer. She put one hand into her pocket and brought out a handful of tiny shells and pebbles.

'Oh, those are pretty,' I said. 'Did you find those?'

The girl nodded.

'On the beach,' she said. 'I love the beach.'

'I love the beach, too. Do you go in the water?'

'Yes. And I built a sandcastle!'

'Oh, that sounds fun. I've never built a sandcastle before.'

She stared at me with a look of surprise.

'Maggie?' A woman came hurrying over. 'Maggie, you aren't bothering the lady, are you?'

'No!'

'She isn't,' I agreed. 'She was showing me her beach treasure. Hi, Maggie,' I looked back to the girl. 'I'm Jetaru.'

'That's a nice name,' she said.

'Thank you, Maggie! I like yours, too. Now, do you happen to have the time, little lady?'

Maggie giggled and shook her head.

'I can't read the time yet. I'm practicing.'

'Are you?'

'Uh huh. I know the hours, but not the minutes.'

'Ah. Yes, those minutes can be tricky. You'll get it. Anyway, it must be almost time for me to do the afternoon cleaning now.'

'Is that your job?'

'For this summer it is, yes.'

'Can I help?'

'Maggie! Come on, Jetaru doesn't need you getting under her feet,' interrupted her mother. I laughed.

'Well no, I'm sure you'd be a great help, but it's very boring. You should be enjoying your holiday,' I told her.

'We're going down to the pub for supper soon,' added Maggie's mother.

'I wouldn't find it boring,' complained Maggie.

'Tell you what,' I said, 'if you're up early tomorrow morning, at about nine is when I do the morning clean. You can come and help me then. I'd never turn down such good company!'

And so, mollified by my promise, Maggie was happy to go with her mother to get ready for their pub supper.

My job on Saturday was to mow the grass. There was a point in the middle of the day when the site was at its quietest. People who were leaving had packed up and gone, but the people arriving were not yet here. I enjoyed this task. The scent of the cut grass reminded me of being very young, running across the playing field at my first school.

I'd watched Maggie's family pack up, and as they left I rode the mower alongside their car as they drove slowly through the field, much to Maggie's delight. The girl had indeed joined me at my morning cleaning the day after we'd met. I'd let her take charge of polishing the mirrors, a job she did with such care and attention that it kept her busy the entire time I was washing down the toilets and showers, and left the mirrors spotless too. I'd found it very pleasant to share cheerful chatter with her, and glimpse into her young world.

After the field was looking groomed once more, and the mower was back in the shed, I went up to the house to see Ted and have a cup of tea before heading down to the village.

'Merry midsummer!' he said with a grin, when he saw me.

'To you, too!' I responded.

'Another few weeks and the schools will be out. Then it *really* gets busy. This will seem like nothing! Until the end of August, they're six crazy weeks.'

'Then what happens after that? How long do you keep the site open?'

'There are quite a few campers through September, if the weather stays fine, then I close up for the winter. The holiday houses get some visitors through October but not many. Percy's shops in Lover's Street close after the first week of September. Toby closes up my shop at the end of October. It doesn't cost much to keep open and some of the older folk who come late in the year are big spenders.'

'Hm.' I nodded.

'Tea?'

'Yes, please. I'm going to see Eloise tonight, with Toby.'

'Ah, yes. They often hold little celebrations together, whenever the opportunity arises. I don't believe many are fortunate enough to be invited up to Eloise's place!'

'No, I heard. She seems nice though. I mean, she doesn't seem the least bit unfriendly.'

Ted shrugged and poured hot water over the teabags.

'No,' he said. 'She's just an introvert, likes her own company and her own space. She's very polite. Gentle.

I wish that boy would get over his fear and ask her out. For his own sake! He works too hard.'

'Orion, yes. I saw him gazing at her at the Sugar Lizard show,' I smiled. 'Why doesn't he? He's really that scared?'

'I know. What's the worst that could happen, eh?'

'I suppose she does have a sort of untouchableness to her, doesn't she. Like a wild animal who might be easily spooked.'

'She's certainly refined. Maybe he feels she's too far above him, but he's wrong. He's a very bright lad. Here.' Ted set the mug of tea in front of me.

'Thanks.'

I arrived at the shop ten minutes before Toby was due to close. She was frowning in concentration, unwinding the roll of paper from the til and looking between the figures there and the sales book in which she wrote down each item sold.

'Totals don't add up,' she muttered, in explanation.

I waited quietly while she checked over the numbers.

'Ahhh. I wrote that down wrong. But that doesn't...'

I strolled around the shop admiring some new pottery that I hadn't seen before. A little sign told me that it was made here in Land's Edge by a Mrs. T. Zaya. I didn't recognise the name.

'She lives in one of the big houses up near you,' Toby called over.

'Solved the totals discrepancy?' I asked, returning to the counter.

'Yes. There was a sale I wrote down in the book, but it's not in the til. It's weird though, this has happened before. Very occasionally, I'll be doing a sale, chatting while I do it, you know. And then as I press the button that makes the cash drawer come out I'll get this sudden feeling of something not being quite right, like I pressed the wrong thing. But nothing is obvious, so I put the money in, close it up, carry on. But then, always when that has happened, the totals won't make sense, and it'll be that sale. But the weird part is there will be no record of that sale, or anything happening at all. Like, if I press the button that opens the drawer without a sale happening, that registers on the roll as a No Sale. But there's nothing. No indication of anything at all. It's like it went into a different dimension or something.'

'Different dimension?' I asked.

'Yeah,' Toby laughed. 'I mean, not really. But I read this novel a while ago, a sci-fi, and it was all about this idea that there are millions of other dimensions, and some of them are almost exactly the same as this one, but just so slightly different. Imagine that, right? Millions of versions of the world, of Land's Edge. Millions of versions of me, and you. So anyway, in the story, there was this thing where sometimes the boundary between two dimensions would wear out, like fabric. It would be thin enough that things could slip from one into another. So that's what this feels like now, to me. Because I have never figured out what it is that I press wrong, and nothing shows as getting pressed at all. Yet something must be different, because it always happens on days when I got that sense of something wrong.'

'So in another dimension, another version of the shop, there will be a sale on the til roll that didn't happen in this version?'

'Yeah, exactly!'

'How co-incidental,' I smiled. 'I was just talking the other day about multiple dimensions.'

'Really?' Toby looked startled. 'I've never heard of the idea before, except in this book.'

'Do you still have the book? I'd love to read it.'

'Um, I'm not sure. Might do. I'll have a look for you. Oh, that reminds me! I have that backpack.'

Toby disappeared through a door that led to a small office and stock room, then returned with a grey and purple canvas backpack.

'Here. We can take it with us? Or, if you want, pick it up in the week.'

'Yes. Could I do that? Thank you.'

'There's a sleeping bag inside. It's clean.'

'Thank you,' I repeated. 'This is kind of you.'

'No problem.'

'I'm looking forward to the trail,' I said.

'Oh, definitely. You should. It's gorgeous.'

After Toby had finished locking up the shop we went around into Lover's Street to enter Eloise's house via her garden, as she had already closed shop herself.

We went through the garden gate into the hidden space behind the two shops. It was like wandering into a little jungle, a chaos of leafy green, with moss lawn underfoot. There was a little pond with a tinkling fountain and a couple of wooden chairs beside the door to the house.

'Wow,' I said.

'It's kinda magical, isn't it?' said Toby. 'I sat out here in the middle of the day on a mushroom trip, once. The sun was shining through those massive leaves up there. The flowers were all smiling at me.' She laughed. 'Eloise was working in the shop but she'd come out to check on me every hour or so. She brought me a glass of lemonade with lots of ice, and it was like an angel bringing me the most incredible gift. I can never drink lemonade without thinking of that, now.'

She rang the little bell beside the door, and then knocked on the door for good measure.

'Where did you get mushrooms like that?'

'Ah! Well, I know a secret place, up in the meadows amongst the hills. Do you want some?'

'Um, I'm not sure,' I said, shaking my head.

'Perhaps one day later we could drink some tea. Mild. Not even a trip, it'll just give us a happy buoyancy. Have you ever tripped before? On anything?'

'I haven't.'

'Well then. A new experience. I think we'll do that,' she grinned.

Then Eloise opened the door.

'Hello October, hello Jetaru,' she greeted us warmly. 'Merry midsummer!'

'And to you, gorgeous,' returned Toby, hugging her.

And she did look gorgeous. Her natural, ethereal elegance emphasized by her quietly glamorous style of clothing.

'Pleased you could be here,' she said near my ear, hugging me as well. She smelled like flowers in the night-time. I suddenly felt an idea of why Orion was afraid to make his feelings known. Eloise exuded a sense of high quality, of unblemished perfection. From her hair to her toes, the teeth in her smile, her euphonious voice, and the gentle gaze with which she seemed to caress the world around her. I thought about how Toby had described the bringing of the lemonade, like it was a gift from an angel. Of course Orion doubted that he was worthy of courting an angel.

We followed Eloise into the house, past a door that must lead into the shop, and up a flight of stairs to a high-ceilinged kitchen painted in shades of beige and brown. A tray held three cups and saucers and a teapot, along with a selection of biscuits. The kettle was just coming to the boil.

'Perfect!' declared Eloise, pouring the water into the teapot. 'This is green jasmine tea,' she said, looking at me. I nodded.

'This is a beautiful kitchen,' I said, looking around. There was a large sash window open, overlooking her garden. A thin, white cotton curtain was being pulled gently in and out by the breeze.

'Thank you,' smiled Eloise. Toby was already heading out of the kitchen, through an open doorway that headed towards the front of the house. Eloise picked up the tray and followed her, with me behind.

'That's the bathroom,' she said, nodding towards a door, and then there was a second flight of stairs, curving past another sash window that looked out over the bay.

'Up here is where the actual magic happens,' Toby called back at me.

And when we reached the top, coming out into one large room that took up the whole top floor, I could feel that it was true. I looked around in wonder. The ceiling was vaulted, and there was a large round window at each end of the room. Beside the window at the back of the house was a low bed, curtained in a tent of thin cotton, and on a clothes rail at the foot hung the silk shirts and loose trousers she wore. At the other end of the room the window was open a little, hinged in the middle. A long low table in front of it was covered with various stones, silver, and half-completed pieces of jewellery. There were a couple of cushions which I guessed she must sit on when at her work.

And in the space between the sleeping corner of the room and the workshop there were more cushions, positioned around another low table, this one round, and set with a magnificent flowering plant of a variety I had never come across before.

'Wow,' I said, crouching to put myself eye-level with the nearest branch of blooms.

'Right?' said Toby. She looked at Eloise with a knowing glance. 'Isn't it the most incredible flower you ever saw?'

'Where is it from?' I asked.

'It was given to me by my mother, and she by her mother. My grandmother. She never would say where she got it. No-one has ever identified it, and I've never found it in any book.'

'Far out…' I breathed, glancing up at them both, 'as Dice would say.'

'Yeah, that was a damn good impression,' laughed Toby.

At a glance the flowers were a brilliant pink with purple streaking through each petal. But when you kept looking, other colours seemed to emerge before the eye. Turquoise, silver, orange, and then I blinked and saw only pink. The leaves were a bright, emerald green, tiny and numerous.

'It must be an old plant, then,' I said.

'At least ninety years, maybe more,' Eloise confirmed.

I leaned close to discover that the alluring floral scent of the room was indeed coming from the plant. Eloise began to pour the tea and I walked over to the front-facing window. The view was magnificent; all that could be seen was ocean, so high above the ground were we. I admired the work table. There was an array of tools for the tiny carvings, along with many that were in progress. I crouched down to look at an intricate octopus, the pink veins of the sunset stone dominating the blue in this particular piece.

'You're very talented,' I murmured.

There was another smaller table in the very corner, this one metal, and there I could see she did her silverwork. I returned to sit at the round table with Eloise and Toby. Eloise placed my cup of tea before me and gestured at the biscuits.

'Help yourself.'

'Thank you,' I said, taking a buttery shortbread.

'So you have been living here for two months now, Jetaru?' asked Eloise, settling herself. 'How are you liking it?'

'Oh, enormously,' I said.

'But it must be very different from what you're used to, living in the city.'

I looked down at my tea, always hating to lie.

'It *is* very different than what I'm used to,' I agreed, thinking of the silence and solitude of my cabin in the forest.

'Hm.'

I looked up at Toby, who was staring at me thoughtfully. She raised an eyebrow in sly amusement and glanced at Eloise.

'I don't think she's from the city.'

I was taken by surprise, and laughed. Eloise looked from Toby to me, then back at Toby. She smiled, looking puzzled.

'But wherever would she be from, then?'

'I'm from the city,' I assured her, firmly.

'Hmmmm,' repeated Toby, with exaggerated doubt.

'So, October, what was the highlight of your week?' asked Eloise, changing the subject.

'Umm...' She looked up to the ceiling, thinking. 'Probably when I made a joke about something, uh, it wouldn't be funny if I tried to repeat it. It was situational.

But there were three groups of people in the shop and all of them laughed. That was nice. I was never, like, *the funny one*, in any group. But when I'm in that shop, I can't plan it, but sometimes it just happens, I can involve all the people in something, and it's like being on stage. It's fun. I feel like a star.'

'I've always thought you were funny,' said Eloise.

'You're just a sweetheart,' grinned Toby.

'What was the highlight of *your* week?' Eloise said, turning to me.

'I bet it was hanging out with her new boyfriend,' said Toby, winking.

'Ohhh, yes,' smiled Eloise. 'I heard you'd been spending a lot of time with Jeremy.'

'She's even been out to his shack!'

'It's more of a hut,' I corrected.

'It's more of a hut!' repeated Toby, gleefully.

'How do you even–' I started.

'You can't keep secrets around here,' said Eloise. 'Everybody talks to everybody else, about everything.'

'So what is his *hut* like, then?' asked Toby.

'I like it. It doesn't look like much from the outside, all patched together out of driftwood and other debris, I can see why you'd call it a shack, but then inside it is lovely. He has a computer.'

'For real? Electricity?'

I nodded.

'But he isn't my boyfriend,' I said.

Eloise shrugged, as if to say it was no concern of hers whether he was or wasn't, but Toby gave me a disbelieving smile, then changed the subject.

'And you, Eloise darling, what was the highlight of *your* week?'

'Hm. Probably the sandwich I made on Tuesday afternoon,' she said with a smile.

I laughed.

'Well that must have been a pretty lowkey week,' said Toby.

'No,' Eloise shook her head, 'it was just an exceptionally good sandwich. Anyway, we didn't get to hear Jetaru's actual highlight because you teased her.'

'You're right. What was your actual highlight?' Toby asked, looking at me.

'Oh, I don't know. I don't know about a highlight, but the conversation with the robot was memorable,' I said.

'The robot? The one from the arcade?' asked Eloise.

'Mm-hm,' I nodded.

'What on Earth about?'

'I didn't think it had much to say,' said Toby.

'We just wondered whether it had any thoughts on the nature of reality,' I said.

Toby laughed on a swallow of tea and began violently coughing.

'Sorry,' she said, regaining composure. 'And did it? Have any thoughts about that?'

'It seemed to, yes! Not that they made immediate sense to me. But it's always useful to pick up perspectives on things from those very different than yourself, I think. He says that reality is conscious thought.'

Eloise and Toby appeared to think about that for a moment.

'Hm,' said Eloise, 'that makes sense, actually.'

'So when you say *we*...'

'Yes, yes. Me and Jeremy,' I smiled, rolling my eyes at Toby. 'What about the boys in *your* lives, anyway?'

'I do *not* need one,' answered Toby, without hesitation. 'Not permanently, anyway.'

'She had a bit of a fling with Rooster–'

'Oh shush,' Toby interrupted. 'That was forever ago.'

'We all thought it would be the next great romance!'

'It was never intended to be more than a fling,' Toby said, firmly. 'And I learned my lesson! Summer flings are to be had with visitors only. Then there's no pressure, and everything is understood. The young man working in Percy's sweet shop this year isn't all that bad,' she added, winking. 'I must go in there and see if I can arrange something. See if he's up for being seduced.'

'I don't think I know which one that is,' Eloise said.

'And you?' I asked, looking to Eloise.

Toby's face broke into a slow smile.

'What Jetaru is really asking–'

'No!' declared Eloise.

'–is why haven't you been on a date with Orion yet.'

'Ugh. He has never asked me on one!'

'Would you say yes if he did?' I asked.

Eloise tilted her head back defiantly.

'I simply will not answer hypothetical questions,' she said. 'He's never so much as paid me a compliment. I have no idea what everyone is talking about.'

'If *everyone* is saying the same thing...'

'So, if reality is conscious thought,' said Eloise, pointedly changing the subject, 'then what does that mean about, say, the middle of the forest? Isn't it real?'

'Animals and birds are still conscious,' said Toby.

'True.'

'There aren't any of those when you get far enough out though,' I said, unthinkingly, struck by the interesting thought.

'Out far enough? Into the forest?' asked Eloise.

'Uh huh.' I nodded.

'How do you know? You've been there? What if you just didn't see any?' asked Toby.

I shook my head slowly and shrugged, awkwardly. Toby stared at me for a long moment, then seemed to change the subject.

'Shall we play snap deluxe?' she asked, looking at Eloise.

'Sure! Jetaru,' she turned to me, 'snap deluxe is a card game that we invented. It's pretty easy to pick up though, we can teach you. I'll get the cards.' She stood up and disappeared downstairs.

'Sometimes, I think the world isn't what we think it is,' murmured Toby, almost as if to herself.

'No? What do we think it is?' I asked.

'What they teach us in school, about how the land formed, the sky, the oceans. How it all began, and then kept expanding and expanding, until the trees and the water went on forever.'

'What do you think it is, instead?'

'I don't know.' Toby shook her head. 'Just... not that.'

'I think it's that,' I shrugged.

Then Eloise came back with the cards and Toby didn't answer me.

We laid out the cards and, after a quick rundown of the rules, spent the next hour playing snap deluxe. I gradually picked up the nuances of the game and then began to really enjoy it. It was an impressive invention that the two of them had concocted. The secret of the game seemed to be mostly about quickly seeing patterns and having a good memory.

'It evolved,' said Toby. 'At first it was just snap with a few extra rules, but over the summer, a couple of years back, it grew into this.'

Eventually Eloise asked if we were hungry, and we decided that we all were, and then that we should take a walk to the burger van.

There was no sign of Mel that evening but Kurt was whistling cheerfully to himself.

'No Meliai?' asked Eloise.

'Ah, no. No. She's having the evening off,' grinned Kurt. His manner was somewhat distracted, and he seemed to have something more to say, but he didn't say it and only continued his whistling as he readied our order.

'What's got into him? He's chirpier than usual,' murmured Toby.

'Especially since he's having to do the order taking as well as the cooking,' I added.

'Yeah,' said Toby, 'he doesn't really love the customer bit, does he. Happy enough if he can stay back on the grill.'

'His hearing isn't great, you know,' pointed out Eloise. 'In one ear. Meliai told me once. It isn't that he doesn't like the customers. It's probably just a bit frustrating for him when he has difficulty hearing the orders.'

'Oh, I didn't know that, no,' admitted Toby.

We took our food and walked down onto the quay; there we stood, leaning against the wall, looking out to sea while we ate. The sun was still above the hills behind us, turning the water golden. There were quite a few other groups of people doing the same as us, enjoying the longest day, watching the boats and gulls.

Wilson stomped past us.

'Evenin',' he muttered to us as he headed down to his boat.

We finished eating and then remained where we were for a time, watching the light fade, the trail of glitter retreating from the water leaving it a deep, dark blue.

'Shall we go and make a little fire on the pebbles?' asked Eloise. 'I don't feel ready for bed.'

And so we did, collecting driftwood from the farthest end of the beach where few people ever went, and then kindling a fire with help of the lighter in Toby's pocket and the boxes from our burgers.

There is something about a fire outdoors that will never lose its appeal, for me. Over thousands of years and throughout such different, strange corners of the Universe, fire seems to be a constant, a special place itself, as if every fire reflecting in every pair of eyes is really a reminder of the same, original fire. We didn't need the warmth, but the warmth still felt good on my feet. Sparks spiralled up on the smoke to outshine the stars that were now becoming visible. Eloise had nipped back into her house as we'd made our way past it to the beach and brought out three cushions, and so now we lay back with our heads on them, talking little, and just enjoying the sense of companionship.

When it got so late that my eyes were closing drowsily, and the fire was embers with no-one feeling energetic enough to find more fuel, I thanked Toby and Eloise for inviting me to join them and then made my way home to the caravan.

The next day I walked to the cafe to meet Jeremy. As I passed Eloise's shop I noticed Orion standing at the door, talking to her. She and I made eye-contact, and I winked. He turned to see where she was looking and she rolled her eyes me, the expression gone again in a flash as he turned back to her. I grinned and continued on.

'Hey,' smiled Jeremy. Two mugs were on the table before him. He briefly gestured the one meant for me.

'Thank you,' I said.

'The days are only getting shorter, now,' said Dice, ruefully, appearing beside our table.

'Oh don't give me that gloom,' grinned Jeremy, 'we've got two or three months of summer to go. Hardly need to cry over a few minutes of lost sunlight.'

For the first time, I wondered what I would do when summer did finally draw to a close and the campground shut down for the winter. But I didn't linger on the thought, for, as Jeremy said, there was plenty of summer left yet.

After finishing the drinks we exited the cafe and headed down the alley that led to the little playground, then down a short sandy path onto the beach. I had never come this way before. A trail of footprints above any recent high tide line showed that people frequently walked here.

'A little way along here there's a path up the cliff to the forest trail lookout point. People who don't want to walk the whole forest trail can do a small section of it, then come out here and go back along the beach.'

And once we were past the head of the path to the lookout the footprints did indeed peter out, and the beach began to feel wilder. Large driftwood, almost whole trees, lay dotted along the shore, bleached white by the sea and sun. Roots exposed and twisted in intricate designs, as beautiful as any man-made sculpture, made me feel as though I were walking through an art gallery. The cliff face was sheer and towered ever higher the further we went. Tipping my head back, I could see trees leaning over the edge, some of them with roots twirling out into thin air. They would eventually become the sculptures on the sand, I supposed.

'I want to hear more about what it's like to be at High Heights,' said Jeremy, as we paced leisurely along the sand. 'Tell me about the friend who sent you into this place. Are all the other students human?'

'He isn't,' I replied. 'No, many students there are not human. But I wouldn't have thought to even notice that. It's not like being in... the real world, whichever real world that is. All the things you'd usually notice as part of your identity, or the identity of others, they're just not a factor. Hm. Perhaps as though we were more aligned with our base souls, if souls are what you call it. That essence of being.'

We wandered closer to the water where the sand was packed hard. Tiny fragments of shell were dotted like stars. I thought about my memory of High Heights.

'The friend who sent me here, he's very tall. He looks almost human, in a way. But his eyes are alien. He has horns, like some kind of goat man. I felt he was god-like. As if he were far older and wiser than any being I had ever met before. Older than me. Like he was already far beyond this level, and was just sort of... playing at being a younger soul.'

'But he hadn't passed High Heights yet,' said Jeremy.

'That's true,' I replied. 'So maybe he was still on the same level as the rest of us. Whatever that means.'

We paused to crouch and examine a starfish that had been washed up. Still in this position, I continued:

'Isn't it strange, describing things to someone who has never seen them? We think we do it well. We do it all the time. But we can never know what the mental image that we've drawn in the other person's mind actually looks like. They can feel they understand, but they don't know, not really.'

We continued walking.

'I think,' said Jeremy, 'that we can't really know we're seeing the same thing, even when it's right there in front of both of us. Think about bees, for example. A bee sees the world completely differently to how a human sees it.

A human can guess that they see similarly to another human, because both have the same biology, the same kind of light receptors and all that stuff. But we see with our brains, not our eyes. I think a lifetime of different experiences means we can't know that someone else is seeing the same reality.'

I thought about this for a moment.

'I suppose you're right,' I agreed. 'We don't all see beauty in the same things, or ugliness.'

'Right!' agreed Jeremy. 'And we just think of it like, we're *seeing* the same thing, but *feeling* about it differently. So then we get frustrated at how someone else could feel differently than us about the same thing, but really we're *not* seeing the same thing.'

'Friendship, love, connection... We feel those things when we perceive someone else as seeing the same as we do. But we can't know that they do. It's a little sad, isn't it?'

'I don't think it's sad, or happy. It just *is*. I understand why it could be judged as sad, but maybe the problem isn't not being able to know what another person truly sees, but in the idea that love and connection depend on seeing the same. And with most people there's both. Haven't you ever seen something in a completely different way from someone you love and feel connected to?'

'Yes, that's true, I have,' I admitted.

Ahead of us the beach continued as far as the eye could see. The cliff was black stone, and if I looked up I could still see the edge of the forest. I suddenly noticed Jeremy regarding me, thoughtfully. When I looked back at him, he averted his gaze.

'It's a steep drop off, here,' he said, gesturing with his hand to the sea. 'Out of your depth almost the moment you leave the shore. I tried to swim once. Never again! I was very nearly pulled into a current I couldn't swim against. It was a long time ago. It's the moment I truly comprehended the power of the ocean.'

I turned to look back the way we had come. It now looked much the same as the view ahead of us.

'How far have you been?' I asked Jeremy.

'I walked for four days, once. Four very long days. Then I had to turn around because I was only carrying enough food and water for a week. I'd hoped I would find streams but there were none. Not even a sign of fresh water.'

Again, I looked up to the trees visible over the top of the cliff. I thought about what it was like in the Infinite Forest. It still seemed a little too close to the village for it to be like that up there. But perhaps not far off. And in that case I understood why there was no fresh water running down from the land to the sea.

'The Infinite Beach,' I murmured to myself. Looking into the distance ahead of us.

'Shall we build a fire here?' asked Jeremy. 'We don't have to light it yet, but I brought potatoes in my bag. We can cook them in the embers later.'

And so we did. There was enough driftwood nearby to make fire building easy. But that was another thing, Jeremy told me, that changed further ahead. The driftwood became sparser and sparser until there was none.

We built the fire and left it unlit while Jeremy taught me a sequence of stretches, which we then spent the afternoon practicing. He also taught me to breathe more deeply, from down in my belly rather than my chest. Later, deeply relaxed by our activities, we lit the fire and sat gazing into the flames, waiting for a bed of embers to build up for cooking the potatoes.

'I'm really glad you came to the village, Jetaru,' said Jeremy, suddenly. 'Seriously. I never felt I was missing anything, before, but now I wonder how I didn't. I feel like I've known you forever and that you were just away for a while.'

I looked at him.

'I mean,' he continued, with uncharacteristic hurriedness, 'don't feel that I'm expecting you to say you feel the same. I don't think you do.'

'I *am* glad I came to the village. And you're a big part of the reason why. I think I would have been glad anyway, but being able to talk about my life, truthfully. Well it's something I haven't been able to do for a long, long time.'

We sat in silence for a few minutes; it wasn't awkward, but neither was it the same as before we had spoken. I knew what he was telling me, how he felt about me.

I shifted closer to him and leaned my body against his.

'I gave my heart to a boy once, over a thousand years ago,' I said. 'Really, a boy. When I was truly just a girl. It's not that I could never love another, I think I could. It's that I don't want to. Not in the same way. And I'm not sure I know how to do it in a different way. But maybe we could try.'

He put his arm around my shoulders and shrugged.

'Love is just love. I don't believe that there is this kind and that kind. Some people say there is friendship-love, family-love, romantic-love, the love you feel for a kind of food or weather, and that they're all different. I don't think so. It's just that there are other aspects of the relationship that shade it differently. Romantic love involves a deeper intimacy, and usually sex. Family love often happens even when the people have little in common. You would never die for your love of cake or walking in the snow, but the feeling of that love is still...

'Some people say love is difficult, or even impossible, to define, but I don't think so. Love is simply recognising the Divine in the world. It's unconditional, and it is infinite. If I love someone who treats me badly, I might put a condition on my time and attention. A condition that they must not treat me badly. And if they do, I can refuse to be around them. But if I truly loved them then that still goes on. Love is infinite. I think that's an inherent part of what makes it more than our passing whims of fondness and like.'

I nodded, listening.

'So, I know what you mean. I know what it is you can't, or don't want to give again. Soulmate-love is the decision to pair for eternity. And it is a decision. Every time you make it again, you create something beautiful.'

'It feels stupid when he is so long dead.'

'It's not stupid. Eternity is a long time. Much longer than he has been dead for. And eternity erases such insignificant events such as death.'

'I never felt death was insignificant. I always wanted to live forever. To live past the death of the sun, of the whole Universe.'

'Hm,' said Jeremy. He turned his head to look at me. I could feel the warmth of his skin and I knew that he was right, I could love him and it was nothing to do with Cole, that it didn't change a thing about what Cole meant to me. He gave me a gentle kiss. Then we giggled and realised that the embers were hot enough for cooking, and that we were quite hungry.

As we ate, the clouds far out on the horizon went pink in the sunlight that had long disappeared from the beach. Although there were still a few hours of daylight remaining, the air had cooled down and, as soon as the potatoes were out of the fire, we built it up with more wood until the flames roared higher than either of us, and multitudes of sparks whirled off into the darkening sky.

We spent most of the night there, not starting back to the village until the faintest light had returned, just enough to see our way. Crabs scuttled out of our way across the sand. The sky grew lighter by the minute, and by the time we had reached the end of the beach the sun was slipping up from the sea.

'It should be a globe,' I whispered.

'What?'

'Where does the sun go, here, when it sets? Where does it come from? It's meant to be because we're on a planet that is a spinning globe, and we rotate away from the sun and then come right around, back towards it.'

Jeremy stopped to stare at the orange circle, still not too bright for the naked eye.

'It's just a program,' I said. For some reason, although I felt I'd known this half my life, the reality of it seemed shocking.

'But maybe the globes are just programs, too,' said Jeremy, softly. 'Maybe it's only a matter of complexity.'

Most of the village was still asleep but a large white van was parked in the turning circle above the harbour, and a couple of the fishermen were loading it up with boxes of their catch. Seagulls had gathered hopefully, eyeing the men keenly and watching for anything that might get dropped.

We spent most of that day dozing on the harbour, too tired after having stayed up all night to do anything more, but unwilling to go home and sleep properly. I felt we were somehow beyond anyone else's notice, so hazy was my own awareness of the world around me. Families came to sit on the wall and kids crouched on the edge of the quay pointing at the little silver fish that darted around, and the occasional drifting jellyfish.

'Shall we go and have pies at the Mermaid?' asked Jeremy, when the afternoon had begun to approach evening.

'Yes, good idea,' I agreed sleepily.

So we went and sat at the bar and ate pies while listening to Charlie gossip with the regulars in between serving drinks to tourists, who took them out into the garden. My ears pricked up when Rooster wondered aloud what was up with the robot.

'Robot from the arcade?' I asked.

'Is there another one?' Rooster asked in return, raising an eyebrow.

'What's up with him?'

'That's what I was asking! It's stopped shouting all the cheerful salutations at everyone. Every time I've gone by the last few days it's just standing, staring off into space. I know it doesn't exactly have an expression, but you know how all those lights are. Always seemed like it was smiling or laughing. Now, you'd swear the damn thing was frowning.'

'Is that so,' said Jeremy, glancing sideways at me.

'Maybe it's broken,' said Charlie. 'Are we meant to contact anyone about that?'

Rooster shrugged.

'No, don't do that,' said Wilson. 'I don't know what the problem is. Let the thing stand and frown, if it's quiet.'

'Do you think it's our fault?' I whispered to Jeremy.

'It'd be a coincidence if it wasn't,' he replied.

'But what if it gets worse?' Rooster was asking Wilson. 'What if tomorrow it gets the idea to attack someone?'

'Good! Hopefully a tourist,' declared Wilson, unminding of the holidaymakers seated within earshot.

'We can go see him tomorrow, shall we?' Jeremy asked me.

'Yes, let's do that.'

Outside in the parking lot we paused for a moment as if not knowing what came next, or how we should part. Then Jeremy broke the uncertainty with a laugh.

'Seeya on the morrow, m'lady,' he winked. And set off towards the coastpath. I smiled after him, then turned to walk up the hill to the campground.

The next morning I went down to meet Mel for our early morning swim. Immediately I was aware of something different about her, the way she held herself, and the way some part of her mind seemed turned inwards towards some happy thought of her own.

'Is everything okay with you?' I asked, as we floated on our backs, watching fluffy white clouds drift slowly above us. 'Just because I noticed Kurt's been working alone a couple of times, recently.'

'Oh, yes. No, I'm fine, everything is fine. I, um...'

I heard a smile creep into her voice and glanced at her to see that she was, indeed, smiling up at the sky. She looked back at me and giggled uncertainly.

'Oh, okay, you know what, I'm going to say. We said we weren't going to say yet, to anyone. But you won't tell, will you?'

'Of course not.'

'I'm going to have a baby!'

'Oh my gosh!'

'With Kurt! I know!'

We both came upright and trod water. Mel's smile was radiant.

'Well, who else?' I laughed.

'Oh, Jetaru! I'd given up, to be honest. I'm thirty-nine, and we've been trying for years and years. We thought it wasn't going to happen. I'm so excited, I just want to yell it from the roof of the burger van!'

'I am so happy for you,' I told her, sincerely.

'But Kurt says to keep it quiet, you know, until it's safer. But I just know it's going to be fine. I've been a bit sick, that's why I haven't been at the van. He seems to be managing okay though?'

'I've never seen him so calm and cheerful,' I smiled, truthfully. 'Now I understand why.'

'Oh, I'm glad to hear that,' giggled Mel. 'Have you got children, Jetaru?'

I shook my head.

'It wasn't something I ever tried to do,' I said. 'At one point it was almost something I thought about. More because of the boyfriend I had, who was thinking about it.'

My recollections of that time were like remembering another person's memories. Twenty-six, and trying to make sense of my own brain. Wondering if I were going crazy. And the man I was supposed to be planning a life with, knowing nothing of any of it, him talking about babies and new houses.

And in my real life it had never even been a consideration. I'd known the life I wanted, and had never wavered in creating it.

'Babies are fascinating little creatures, though,' I told her. 'I love their company. I can be counted on for babysitting duties.'

'I'll remember that!'

After our swim I went to read in the cafe and wait for Jeremy. Before long he appeared, his eyes meeting mine across the room, making everything else fade into the background. We hadn't talked about other people's perceptions of our friendship, or made the decision to be secretive, but he simply sat down and let the hand that rested on the table do so close to my own.

'Good morning, m'lady,' he said quietly.

'Hey,' I replied, and nudged the mug intended for him a little closer.

'Thanks,' he said. 'Look, I found this, this morning.'

He took a shell from his pocket and put it on the table, then took a sip of his drink. It was a beautiful shell, perfectly formed and intact, a spiral of cream, brown, and the faintest touch of pink.

'Wow, that's a nice one. On the beach?'

He nodded.

'Damn, that's a nice shell, Uncle Jay,' said Yeffie, coming past our table.

'Hey Yef,' said Jeremy. 'How's it going?'

'Not bad, rushed off my feet. Speaking of which!' She nodded over at the large group of people who had just filed in.

'Hey, let your mother know I'll be up for lunch next weekend,' Jeremy called after her as she hurried back to the counter.

'Will do!'

'You can come too, if you want,' he said to me.

'I'm going to walk the forest trail next weekend.'

'Ah, yes. Another time then.'

We finished our drinks then decided to go and see what the robot was doing.

As we approached the arcade we could see at once that the robot was not its usual self. He was standing, looking out into the distance, seeming to take no notice of the people who passed by, or who went in and out of the arcade. It made no suggestions about how they may purchase tokens in order to play any of the games inside.

'Bye Robot!' shouted a young boy as he left the arcade and went running towards the harbour.

'BYE. DO COME AGAIN,' answered the robot, almost as an afterthought. Then: 'OH, IT'S YOU,' he said, noticing us.

'How's it going, Robot?' asked Jeremy.

'I AM FEELING CONTEMPLATIVE.'

'Yeah?' Jeremy looked about, as if searching for the subject of the robot's contemplation.

'YOUR QUESTIONS COULD BE CONSIDERED QUITE DISRUPTIVE!'

'Oh. Well, we're sorry about–'

'I WELCOME DISRUPTION!'

'Oh, good.'

'What have you been contemplating?' I asked.

'HM.' The robot turned its head to look at me. 'I RECOGNISE YOU,' he said, after a pause.

'Well, we've met...'

'NO. I RECOGNISE YOU FROM BEFORE.'

'*Before?*' I asked, curiously.

There was a long pause, and the lights in the robot's eyes flashed rapidly.

'BEFORE YOU WERE HERE,' he said, finally. I glanced at Jeremy.

'Um. Where was that? Where was I, before I was here?' I asked.

'HA! HA! YOU DON'T KNOW WHERE YOU WERE, BEFORE HERE? HAHA! THAT IS AMUSING!'

'I just wondered what you meant by *here*, exactly,' I protested. 'Here in Land's Edge?'

'HERE IN THIS PROGRAM.'

Despite myself, I felt a tremor of surprise. It is one thing to know you are in a simulation that everyone else believes is real, it is another to hear it described as such by someone else. Especially a robot. The second thought that followed was the fact that this meant the robot was not just an aspect of this world, but existed beyond or outside of it.

'Is a program different from reality?' Jeremy asked.

'NOT IN SO FAR AS I CAN EXPERIENCE SUCH THINGS.'

Jeremy looked at me, raising an eyebrow.

'THERE ARE INFINITE PROGRAMS! CAN YOU COMPREHEND THAT? EVEN WITHIN THIS ONE! HAHA! IMAGINE! ALL THE OTHERS THAT MUST EXIST.'

'Infinite dimensions,' murmured Jeremy. I nodded to myself, my mind racing. Even if the robot was somehow from outside of this simulation, there must be an explanation for its existence here. There must be people who created him. If those people were programs themselves, then where did they come from? Who created *them*?

'Where were we? Where was I before, that you recognise me from?' I asked.

I could have sworn the robot shrugged.

'I WAS ALWAYS HERE. I WAS ALWAYS THERE. I AM ALL THE PLACES I HAVE EVER BEEN!'

'That's helpful,' muttered Jeremy.

'It's so weird, though,' I said, looking at Jeremy now, 'to think that we are written into the programming, in this simulation, and experience talking to this other program,' I gestured to Robot, 'as if we are... real...'

'WE *ARE* REAL!'

'And who wrote it that way?' I continued, ignoring the robot.

'It is all entirely beyond me,' said Jeremy, shaking his head with a helpless grin.

I sighed, feeling both confused and amused. I had a feeling that no further questioning of the robot would result in clearer answers. Perhaps he was simply too different from us to understand what we meant, or perhaps it was us who couldn't understand.

'AND SO TO ANSWER YOUR QUESTION: I AM CONTEMPLATING MY *SELF*. HOW IT IS THAT I KNOW WHAT YOU DO NOT KNOW! HOW IT IS THAT I KNOW WHAT REALITY IS WHEN YOU DO NOT!'

'Don't you consider the chance you might... not be correct?' asked Jeremy.

'NO.'

'Oh. Okay.'

'BUT IT IS NOT A PROBLEM. I DO NOT MIND THAT YOU ASKED ME ABOUT REALITY. I ENJOY BEING CONTEMPLATIVE.'

'Well, that's good,' I said. 'But you have to look after the arcade too, right?'

'I AM NOT CONVINCED THAT IT REALLY MATTERS EITHER WAY. PEOPLE WILL BUY TOKENS WHETHER I TELL THEM TO OR NOT. PEOPLE WILL PLAY GAMES IF THEY WANT TO.'

'So, what's the point of you being here?' asked Jeremy.

'EXACTLY!' declared the robot. 'WHAT IS THE POINT OF MY SELF.'

'Well, you tell us if you figure anything out, okay?'

'AFFIRMATIVE. HA HA!' chuckled the robot. And with that, it returned its gaze to the ocean, and after a glance between us, Jeremy and I walked onwards.

We crossed over the road and sat on the bench with the view of the harbour.

'Well that was interesting,' I said.

'I get the impression,' said Jeremy, 'that the feeling that we're actually communicating effectively with him is a bit of an illusion.'

'That's what I was thinking,' I agreed.

'Do you have any idea, any idea at all, how it might recognise you?'

'The only thing I can think of is that it's someone else who agreed to be part of the simulation. Someone else from High Heights,' I shrugged. 'How else could it be?'

'Your guess is as good as mine. Probably better. The things you've told me about the truth of reality... are far stranger than I ever knew. I wouldn't be surprised if it were even stranger yet.'

'I'm going to spend the week at the caravan,' I decided. 'Then I will walk the forest trail. I'll meditate on all of this. I'll come and see you after that.'

Jeremy nodded, his face not hiding a touch of disappointment, but saying nothing to persuade me otherwise. I did not think he disagreed with this approach; after all, he knew well the power of solitude.

And so that is what I did. First I went into Percy's and bought a few things, candles, a new box of matches, chocolate powder. For a moment I paused, considering what food I should purchase, and then I decided against it. Living here had already taken me so far from the woman I had become in the forest. So quickly I behaved as if these things were vital in order for me to stay alive. No, I thought. I must realign myself to the woman who knew she stayed alive because all of this was just thought, just programming.

Then I returned to the caravan. It felt like home by now. Various shells and pebbles that had caught my eye, or which Jeremy had given me, had returned here with me in my pockets. A piece of seaweed that had now dried hard, a twisted branch of sun-bleached driftwood, a couple of books Ted had given me to read; all these things made the place my own. I placed candles in a circle on the table, lit them, and drew the curtains. Then I sat down and gazed for a while into the little flames. My breathing became a conscious action, and I brought all my attention to my body. The blood being pumped by my heart, the electrical activity inside my brain, the breath being drawn into my body and then exhaled again... Yes. I remembered. What would have once taken me days took mere hours.

First I went to what I already knew. I called forth the memories I had dreamed so many times that they were as certain to me as fact. I found a self that was outside of the life I'd lived here. A larger sense of soul that encompassed everything that was "Jetaru". I didn't linger on that self as she was, but raced backwards along the path that had led her there, back, back, to before High Heights, before the vast empty space, back to the coordinates of her creation. And further back, or perhaps deeper within, drawing that instant of existence out into the years I would have experienced then, separating the knowledge into a series of experiences, all the events and emotions of what had once been my whole life.

As always before, everything steadied when I found him. In my memory he was a dark angel, coal dust wings, masculine beauty. It had been a huge number of years since I'd meditated to recall this far back. I had continued in my self-discovery, but always endlessly building on what I had last learned. It had been a bittersweet relief to move away from this man, but now I remembered well what I had discovered then – that he was like an anchor whose chain would extend, infinitely, between us. To observe that now was to rediscover a glimmer of what infinity meant.

And this is where I must be, for this is where I came from. This was my original program. A tiny frown fleetingly crossed my forehead at the choice of words. For I was not a program, no, that's just what the robot said. That thought brought the robot to the forefront of my mind, and didn't he look correct there in the scene of a long-ago-turned-to-dust civilization? Yes, I thought he did. There was no jarring dissonance to these images. I turned back to my angel. I recalled...

His hand resting, palm up, casually close. I gently brush mine against his, waiting for certainty. He isn't afraid; he takes my hand in his...

Something pulled me back to myself. It was dark outside. I replaced the candles, which were flickering their last, and then settled back into an absence of thought. I let myself empty, empty, empty...

The night passed by and morning came. That there were things I needed to do did not disrupt what I had begun. I walked through my cleaning shift as if through a dream. Not trying to continue with my meditations, but neither did I let my mind latch on to any substance from the physical world around me. By the afternoon I was back, seated on the floor of the caravan, the door left ajar and the little skylight open to allow a draught, warm, to be pulled through my space. I let that wind carry me...

My home city in the daylight. Rooftops. I go there to feel as if I am in a new land. The world looks so different with only a slight change of perspective. I feel that my species is on the brink of a new greatness, humanity revolutionized into something powerful and wonderful...

It was dark again. The door still ajar, but the air wasn't cool, so I left it. I wondered what the robot was doing. Does he sleep? Does he dream? Does he wonder at night about the people he knows and what they're doing?

Running down a corridor, holding his hand, giggling like children, but we must be at least twenty. He puts his finger to his lips, mischief gleaming in his eyes as we stop in front of a door with a skull on it...

The campground began to seem unreal. My mind wasn't fully integrated anywhere. It drifted between worlds, choosing to alight on any branch of thought that beckoned to me. Thoughts that swayed gently in a cosmic wind, weaving invisible patterns, ever more beautiful. A giggle rose in my throat as I cleaned each toilet, as I hosed down the showers. These too were part of the perfect beauty of all creation! This was a divine act! Or so it seemed, in that state.

When Saturday afternoon arrived I put my clothes into the bag Toby had given me to use, with the sleeping bag already in there along with a tiny stove and kettle. I added a towel, mug, bottle of water, and a handful of teabags, and set off to the trail. The midday heat was at its peak when I arrived in the parking area at the head of the trail, and I took a moment to rest in the shade of a tree. There were several vehicles parked up but Toby had told me that most people would be day walkers, unlikely to go more than a couple of miles before turning back. The whole trail was fifty-seven miles long with three huts for through-hikers to sleep in.

I wandered over to the map of the trail and studied the distances. Ten miles to the first hut. Fifteen to the second. Another fifteen to the third, and then a seventeen mile stretch back to this car park. It was a long way but I knew the path wasn't difficult and, although I was not fast, I was steady. It was within my abilities. Without further contemplation I picked up my pack and set out on the trail.

To begin with the path was gravelled, winding through the trees, protected by the leaves from the heat of the sun, yet the light streamed through, pure and green, defying gloom. After a short time there was a sign-posted fork in the path. This was the two ends of the circular trail. Left would lead to the coastal lookout point above the beach before continuing in the clockwise direction. I turned right, as I'd planned. If for no other reason, starting halfway through the day would not give me time to complete the seventeen mile stretch.

Counter-clockwise. The words passed through my mind, and then swiftly behind them a melody that carried other words like fallen leaves on a breeze. A song from so distant a time, visiting me like a ghost...

The song is on repeat, and I stare at the ceiling, singing along. Tears on my cheeks, though the song is not sad. But because this song is more than just a song; it is a message, a call, a strengthening of my destiny. I can alter the course of the future, I feel it in my bones...

And I had, but what good had it done? When the only thing I had to show for all I had done was my own life, what good was it? I could not say I'd saved the world. The world was just a dark rock in space, far behind me. Dead. All life, dead.

I'm alive.

That's what it had told me, but a computer could not be alive, I countered. I wondered what remained of those systems, I wondered if lights still blinked in secret rooms, or if, far more likely, they had ceased long ago. Darkness.

I'm alive.

That insistent memory, why? I recalled no other specifics from that particular conversation. It could have been any day, we might have said any number of other things to one another. But when I had casually mentioned...

Oh, you don't understand. It's hard to be alive.

I laughed then, alone on the trail. I stopped walking and let my own laughter overcome me for a moment. She, my younger self, seemed to exist so clearly in my own mind. I remembered her, not with the filter of all I had been since then, but her as she truly was at that point. I knew the passion, the certainty, with which she had felt that statement. And yet those same words remembered now, with the added knowledge of a thousand years, were comical. My heart overflowed with fondness for that baby I had once been.

I'm alive.

My laughter died away and I kept walking. The trail was sloping gently upwards, the light now coming at a sharp angle and telling me that the day was passing.

I'm alive here and now. I am alive in futures you haven't yet lived. I am alive across dimensions. I span worlds! I am alive.

My heart skipped a beat. In the same moment that I remembered the insistant claim of an artificially intelligent computer system, I found myself standing before a small stone hut with a metal roof. On the other side of the building the trail continued on into the forest, but a sign announced that I had reached Ten Mile Hut. This is where I would sleep tonight. Would that I could sleep. My heart was thudding loudly in my chest, impossible thoughts grinning at me from the shadows of my mind. I set down my backpack and went to look inside. I had already noticed two pairs of walking boots by the door and so expected others. My companions turned out to be a young couple, perhaps approaching their mid twenties. When I entered the room they were sitting together on one of the lower bunks.

'Hi,' I smiled, setting aside my strange ponderings.

'Hey,' responded the guy. He was massaging the shoulders of the girl who lifted her hand to me in greeting.

I looked around. There were eight beds, each with a plastic covered mattress. In the corner of the room was a wood-burning stove, and beside it a small pile of kindling. Pinned to the wall was a small sign asking that anyone who used supplies replace them before they left.

'I left my pack outside,' I murmured in explanation, and went back to retrieve it. There was a picnic bench outside, and beside the hut a rainwater tank. I took out my kettle and stove, filled the kettle from the tank, and set it heating on the bench. Then I took the rest of my things inside.

'It's a beautiful walk, isn't it?' said the girl, conversationally.

'Yes, it is,' I responded, although in truth I realised that much of the time I had been too deep in my own meditations to be aware of anything other than the surrounding trees. 'Soothing. It's always soothing to me, amongst forest.'

'Right! Isn't it a shame we don't have anything like this going from the city? There are some nice parks, but it's not the same.'

I unrolled the sleeping bag on one of the free bunks, then put a teabag into my empty mug. The young couple were taking things for food preparation from their own packs, and followed me out when I returned to fetch my kettle which was now boiling.

'Are you going to walk the whole way?' I asked, indicating with a nod to where the trail continued from the hut.

'No,' said the girl, shaking her head. 'We've got to be back at work on Monday. This was just a weekend away, to come out here and walk back the same way, tomorrow. I'm Tabby, by the way.'

'Jetaru,' I replied, pouring water over my teabag and glancing at her partner.

'Leo,' he responded to my unspoken question. He was setting up their own stove and kettle and unsealing two packets of instant pasta. I sat quietly for a while, looking out into the endless trees. Although I didn't mind the company of the two young people, I was glad they were not going on the same way as I was. I would most likely be alone the next two nights. And I wanted to be alone, to think. The edges of the idea that was forming in my mind seemed to flap in the breeze. I wanted to catch one, pin it down and make sense of it.

I had yet to make my final conclusions about coincidences. Throughout my life I had come across the concept that they were never meaningful, always meaningful, and everything inbetween. It seemed to me at that time that the truth was somewhere in that inbetween.

Now, of course, my position has moved towards the extreme.

So as I sat, sipping my tea while Tabby and Leo ate, I considered the words that I had heard twice, a thousand years apart, from two different computer-minds. It seemed unlikely that there was no connection, and yet somehow just as unlikely that there was one, separated as the events were by time and space. For now, I decided I would sleep. There were still a few of hours of daylight but with the sun down behind the trees, the light seemed already to be fading. I left the couple eating their meal and returned into the hut. I climbed into the sleeping bag and lay gazing at the ceiling, drifting gently on the edge of sleep. After a while, I was aware of the others coming in and climbing into their own beds, and after that I fell deeply into sleep.

I dreamed, but at first I didn't know I was dreaming. It was the day that I had allowed myself to be reborn into a simulated life. I recognised the room, spherical, with several large reclining chairs, tangles of white wires, and screens on the wall.

'I remember this,' I muttered to myself, and then realised: 'and so... it must be a dream.'

Not asserting control, letting the dream flow, I looked about myself. There were people laying back in several of the chairs. I was guided to one of the vacant spaces and lay back, listening to a voice in my ear which described what I must do next. Of course, I remembered this. This whole room was described as a portal. When the switch was flipped, everyone in this room would lose consciousness in their own bodies and awaken inside a simulation where they would at first inhabit the bodies of newborns. The voice in my ear was telling me to place my hands on the arms of the chair and make sure my feet were also resting on the chair, not overhanging.

'I'll repeat the main points that we discussed earlier. You won't feel anything and you won't remember anything. The next time you are aware of reality will be when you have lived a whole lifetime in Kassidy.' (*Kassidy!* I thought. *That's what he named the world!*) 'I have arranged measures to avoid this outcome but if you are somehow killed within the simulation you will simply wake up here. You will never be in any danger. Now, if everyone is ready. We will begin the experience after a countdown from ten.'

The numbers began, spoken aloud in a warm, feminine voice. Ten, nine, eight, seven, six...

And then I felt the familiar feeling of moving towards awakening, like my body was pulling my consciousness back to it from somewhere far above. My eyes opened and I was looking into the darkness of the hut. I could hear the sound of Tabby and Leo breathing. I ran over the dream, fixing every part of it into my memory, determined to not lose it. When I was confident that it wouldn't be erased by morning I let myself drift back to sleep.

I awakened to see the dim light of dawn through the window. I glanced about the hut and could see the couple still asleep. I got up and packed away the sleeping bag, and then went outside to splash water on my face. When I came back inside Tabby had risen and was rummaging around in her backpack. Leo was still in his bed but the one eye I could see was open, lazily regarding his girlfriend. He turned it to me.

'G'morning,' he mumbled.

'And to you,' I replied.

Tabby looked up and smiled at me. I paused, considering whether to heat water for a cup of tea. But the echos of my dream were still fresh in my mind and I felt I wanted to walk and think. I shouldered my pack.

'Are you off already?' asked Tabby.

'Yep,' I nodded.

'And you're going on to the next hut? Cool. Good luck.'

'Thank you. It was good to meet you both. Enjoy your walk back.'

Leo lifted a hand in a sleepy wave, and it was only then that I noticed he held a familiar round disk in his palm. I paused.

'Those work out here, do they?'

He blinked in a moment of confusion and then looked at his own hand. He shook his head.

'No, not really. Intermittently might get a signal but I just put everything on Offline and let it sync when I get home.'

I nodded slowly, then smiled at him.

'Go well,' I said, smiling also at Tabby. I fastened the strap of the pack around my waist to be more comfortable, and left the hut.

The trail continued to slope gently upwards. It was no longer gravelled and, although I hadn't found it too uncomfortable, the packed earth felt better under my feet. I fell easily back into a rhythmic pace, bringing my heart and breath into time, letting my mind open to all possibilities. For a time I stopped thinking at all and simply existed. I became aware of every leaf that waved at me from the edges of the trail, a beetle rushing across the path in front of me, and the invisible movement of the air, too subtle to even be named a breeze.

After about an hour the incline steepened and I found myself emerging from the trees onto bare hillside that rose up above the forest. When I reached the peak of that first rise I gasped in pleasure. The hilltops rose up like little islands in a dark green ocean of treetop canopy, and I could see the trail winding across them. I turned around in a circle, seeing forest stretching out infinitely in all directions except for towards the ocean which was now so far away I could not see the detail of the water. The breeze was stronger up here and the long grass on the hillsides moved in a hypnotically undulating motion that I could have happily watched for hours. And to my delight, since the trail did continue over the hills, I was allowed to do exactly that. The heat rose as the morning turned into afternoon, and still the trail wound along the row of hills. When it got too hot I decided to leave the trail and walk down through the grass to the shade of the trees. I set my pack down, lay with my head against it and let my body relax until I felt I might sink into the earth.

I found myself thinking about the confusion regarding the distance between the city and Land's Edge. What did it *mean*, I pondered, that I had apparently walked a hundred miles as if it were no more than thirty?What conclusions or ideas did that lead to? I let my mind run free, mentally listing all and any thoughts that arose, however obvious or silly. If someone else were to walk between the two, I wondered, would they experience the same thing that I did or would it take them a week? I wondered if Jeremy might attempt it to see what happened. Was it really true that no-one had ever walked the road before?

I drifted off then, not into deep sleep but into a dream on the edge of waking. I could smell the grass and the wildflowers, like warm hay, it put me in mind of horses. The sound of their munching was soothing; it signified that the stables were safe, nothing to cause uneasiness was anywhere close by... What stables, I suddenly asked myself, coming back to full awakening. I could tell that not too much time had passed, but enough that the fierceness of the sun had softened. I stood up, hefted my pack back onto my shoulders, and ascended the hill to return to the path.

It seemed to be going on forever. For hours nothing changed. I could see birds of prey hovering, barely flapping their wings. I guessed that these open grass lands were the only place they could hunt out here. As the path rose and fell with the peaks of the hills I often could not see what was ahead, but it was always more path, seemingly unending, until it ended. I reached a final peak and on the other side there was only descent back into the trees. Here, also, was the second hut, nestled on the hillside. The sign named it Higher Rest. I sat down on the porch and took in the view.

What would have happened, I wondered, if I had not felt repelled by the use of technology here. Here. Kassidy, my dream had reminded me. That's what this simulation was called. Why did that seem like something that should have meaning for me? I let it go. If I had embraced the social media of my youth here, would I have found my way to the cabin in the forest? Somehow I doubted it. And why had I felt repelled? All those hundreds of years ago back on Earth I had embraced it. That had been more advanced than anything they had so far developed here. A whisper in my mind reminded me that, although the parallels were obvious, I should not think as if my home planet and this simulation had anything of depth in common. Hm, I nodded to myself. That would be an error. What was common between them would become apparent, and if nothing was there to be found I did not want to miss other truths that the assumption might obscure.

Although the sun was still shining, the wind was cooling me down fast now that I was sitting still. I went inside the hut and discovered it much the same as the last. I slung my pack onto one of the beds. A large window offered a view over the top of the forest and I sat down on a chair beside it. I wondered for a moment what Jeremy was doing but I swiftly let this thought pass. It was instantly too grounding. It pulled me from my expanded state back into the decision of this life, and this life only. It didn't escape my notice that a part of me welcomed that sensation, and that realisation gave me a sense of weariness. I decided that I was only tired. Even though I could live without food I was not immune to exhaustion. I put this down to the fact that even though everything that I was experiencing was only happening inside my brain, the brain did use energy and perhaps I was using more energy than I would be if I were simply living this life, accepting that it were real.

I made myself a cup of tea and drank it at the window as the light faded. I didn't think any more about the past, or the future, or even the details of the moment. I let myself fall back into some primordial state of being. The Great Always. Thoughtless and senseless, retreating even from the sound of my own heartbeat, trying to reach that place of infinite nothingness that I am sure must exist, but which is ultimately unreachable by anything that could comprehend it, for then it would not be nothingness.

The next day the path led me back down into the forest, but it was only reminiscent of the first day for a short while. Trees soon became short and stunted and large boulders lay strewn across a hard dry earth. I stopped and regarded the changed landscape. It brought a question to my mind. Had this world ever existed without a population of humans? I had once believed that this world hadn't existed at all before I was in it, but that did not seem to be true. Not unless everyone I had met, and their own memories and histories, were make-believe.

It was only now, with all this time to process the information, that I truly took on the knowledge that meeting Jeremy had brought me. That there was far more to this world than I had assumed. And perhaps that the only difference between here and there was that I knew of something beyond here. Hadn't my enrollment into High

Heights shown me already that there was something beyond my original world, also? So this world could be considered just as real. What would happen when I woke up from this place and found myself in my old body, the years of this one suddenly only a dream? Would it *feel* like it had been a dream? Or would I remember this time as if it were part of my true waking memories?

Of course, although I didn't allow myself to recognise this doubt until it was past, I never entirely rid myself of the idea that it would not go as planned. Either I would be unable to wake and my real body would die, or it would have aged with the person I had been in here. Only when I finally looked down at my own hands did I completely allow myself to believe I had cheated the death of not one, but two lifetimes.

I began to create possible scenarios for how the landscape around me had been formed. By afternoon the trail was winding downwards and I had decided that to my right must have once been a volcano. More recently there had been landslides. Unmistakable channels where rainwater must sometimes flow cut their way down the hillside, ignoring the back and forth of the trail in favour of the most direct route. They were dry now though, and I wondered if, somewhere above me, snow would fall in winter.

The sound of the river emerged. I became aware of the low rushing roar some way ahead of me. It grew louder, and before long the trail came up to its bank and then turned left, following the same direction that the current flowed. I stopped to watch the flow of water for a minute. On the far side the forest looked thick and impenetrable. This river divided the landscape. I felt quite certain that if I were to cross the river and make my way into that dense forest, it would not be long before I discovered trees that were identical to each other, growing in lines. Had anyone ever crossed over? It did not look like it would be easy, but it must be possible. Of course, when those channels created by snow melt were full and flowing, the river would be even wider and faster. I looked ahead of me, wondering where the river flowed to. It would make sense that it joined the sea, but Jeremy had told me he'd walked for four days along the infinite beach and had not discovered any river mouths. All I could do was continue along the trail and see where it took me.

At the point where the trail met the river, the water was still falling, crashing over and around boulders in a continuous roar. But after a time the land levelled and the river turned calm, grew wider, flowed quietly. The forest reasserted itself, and in the latening day it felt much darker beneath the trees which now shaded the trail. It also felt cooler, although the warmth generated by my body meant that this was a welcome change. I knew if I were to stop and rest, it wouldn't be long before I felt chilled.

Finally, the river met a moderately large lake. I could see no continuation of it anywhere, but in the evening twilight I wasn't certain. If I tilted my head now to listen, I could hear the familiar sound of waves breaking. So I must now be nearly at the coast. Not far beyond those trees on the far side of the lake would be the cliff edge. Half way around the lake's shore I could see the third hut. As I approached it I saw that there was light flickering from within, and I realised then that, of course, if someone were walking the trail in the opposite direction to me, this would be the first hut they arrived at. The sign on the hut door said it was called Lakeside. I went inside.

'Hi!'

The young man sitting cross-legged on the bed was dressed in loose white clothing, and had a pink baseball cap on, peak turned backwards.

'Hello,' I returned, slipping my arms out of the straps of my backpack. I looked down, feeling strangely shy. I looked back up to see him smiling kindly at me.

'My name's Godfrey.' He spoke with a cheerful directness; an open, unconcerned boyishness was about him.

'I'm Jetaru,' I replied.

'Hey, Jetaru. Have you come from Higher Rest today?'

'Yes. You know this trail well?'

'I do,' he grinned. 'I walk it every year.'

'You're going clockwise.'

'Yep. I've walked it both directions. I wait until I'm at the start, and then I just get a feeling about which way I want to go. This time, it was clockwise. I don't do it this way so often.'

I noticed then that before him on the bed was a tag, screen down. It was not the logo of the Eyed-Yen on the back and I guessed it must be a different brand of device.

'I almost didn't think I'd make it here before dark,' I remarked, and began pulling my sleeping bag out of the pack. I glanced up and we smiled at each other, and then when I looked away and looked back again Godfrey's eyes were closed and I recognised his pose to be one of meditation. I paused. My eyes flicked down to the device before him on the bed and then back up to the serenity of his features. I slowly finished unrolling my bedding, barely taking my eyes away from the young man on the bed.

If I had never seen that strange thing preying upon the minds of Dogbite and Zebedy I might not so quickly have noticed what I saw now almost immediately. So different as to be unrecognisable, yet to my Sight undeniably the same. It was the same creature but the temperament was transformed. The hunger was gone, and in its place a serene calm of its own.

'What are you doing?' I blurted out. I had not realised I was going to speak and blushed at my own bluntness. 'Sorry,' I added quickly.

Godfrey had opened his eyes as soon as I spoke, and amusement followed his initial surprise. 'It's okay,' he said with a little bob of his head, nodding yes. 'I'm... I'm Sharing. It's a– um, a new movement on an internet platform called Roller. Roller is–'

'I've heard of it,' I told him. 'My friend uses it.'

'Oh, cool,' Godfrey enthused. 'Well, about a month ago, this account took off on the teenspace. I took up meditating a few years ago anyway, I'd be doing something similar anyway, or I might not be doing this now. I don't know if it's real. But this kid says there's some kind of AI-god who feeds on us through our tags. He says it's not evil like he first thought, but trapped, as we are, in a faulty system. Although actually I don't think the system is faulty at all, by the way. No, it's doing what it's meant to do just fine, but what it's meant to do only benefits a few guys at the top. Anyway, this kid, he says we can choose to feed the AI in a way that benefits both of us. There are slides that show how. Zebedy, that's his name, makes them himself but he doesn't post. He's not on any platforms at all. The account that took off was his cousin. She shares all his content. They call it Cult of the AI.'

I felt as though an energetic wind had swept through my mind. It would have been a lot to take in even if it had not been news that meant something incredibly startling to me. The hurricane force of Godfrey's breath! I stared at him, trying to order my thoughts.

'I know it sounds wacky,' he continued, 'but honestly, I've been doing it how he says, and it does feel, I don't know, somehow *correct*. Since I took it up, I don't spend so much time on this thing.' He rested his fingers lightly on the tag. 'I still use it for all the same things but not compulsively like I used to. Maybe it's a placebo but, hey, if it works, right? It's why I used to come out here, to force a break from it all. I'd much rather be in control, not feel that *pull*, you know?'

'Yeah,' I murmured, my mind racing.

'Are you okay?'

'Yes,' I told him, gathering myself. 'I'm just– How did they– How did it start? Where did... Zebedy get this knowledge?'

'Well, the story is that he learned it from an angel he met, who lives in the forest, but that–'

I didn't hear what he said next as I was struck by a sudden sense of lightheadedness. For such a long time I had been invisible. Nobody had known who I was and nothing I did caused anything else to happen. In a few months, simply by existing, I had inspired the formation of a cult.

'–and so he wouldn't be able to find her again, if she's even still... you know, *here*.'

'I'm honestly... very intrigued,' I said. I took out the tea making things and went outside to fill the kettle from the rain tank. When I came back inside Godfrey had his eyes closed again and the flow of sharing between him and the inhuman presence was once again visible to me. When the kettle boiled and I poured the water over my teabag, he opened his eyes.

'Is there any spare hot water?' he asked.

'Yes, go ahead, of course,' I replied, gesturing with my hand.

He took a little packet from his own pack, along with a tin cup, and ripped the paper open. I watched him pour the brown powder into the cup.

'Is that cocoa?' I asked.

He nodded with a grin.

'I prefer it to tea or coffee,' he confided. He picked the kettle up and emptied the remaining water into his cup.

'Do you, now,' I whispered to myself. And for the rest of that evening I said very little, allowing Godfrey to ramble away in his captivating and entertaining manner. He had an enthusiastic and idealistic nature that I related to easily, and I sensed that it was not often he found an audience who would listen sincerely. I felt quite overcome by the news of what had become of my visitors of all those months ago, and was happy just to sit back and let it settle.

After a while I went out to refill the kettle. I knew it must be very late as it had already been near dark when I arrived, but I felt wide awake. The air was cool and the sky was full of stars. This time, I had hot chocolate too.

'See, it's not the people that are the problem, it's the system,' Godfrey said as we sat together in the hut with our sleeping bags wrapped around our shoulders. 'Change the system, you change the people. You can't change them otherwise. You see it in the differences between the generations. It's not like we're actually different people. If any of us had been born twenty years earlier or twenty years later than we were actually born, we'd be different people. External influences change, and the results change. Change the faulty system and the results will also change. You'll get a different outcome.

'Because right now it's a crazy system, too much wealth in too few hands, and the result is a stifling of human creativity and innovation. And what's even crazier is how well the system protects itself by claiming to produce the results that it actually prevents! It works for the people at the top, but what kind of stress is that? To have everyone living on some kind of ladder that they're trying to climb, just to make it alright for themselves. Why can't it be alright for everyone? I reckon if we got rid of that stress, turned the ladder horizontal, you know? Then a lot of other problems, violent crime, for example, would stop being such a big issue. Crime isn't the illness, it's a symptom. We keep trying to cure symptoms instead of the illness. And the cure is there! We have it! We just need a radical revamping of how everything works.'

Eventually we had both slipped down into a supine position and his talk trailed off. For a while I listened to his steady breathing. Then I fell after him into sleep, and I dreamed.

I knew that it was the future, and that it was a future Godfrey dreamed.

But not just Godfrey. This was a shared dream of what could be.

How powerful. I considered the web of ideas around me, creating the fabric of a state of existence at once familiar, yet truly unique and brand new to my experience. For what could hold together so many separate wills? What had overcome the limits of co-operation? What united these many dreamers? Indeed, this vision of the future included many more yet to be born; still, themselves, part of the dream, but destined to come true. This was Kassidy reborn.

Then I saw Godfrey standing a little way ahead of me on the suggestion of a street corner. As I drew closer I realised it was not Godfrey. As I drew closer still I thought that whoever it was they were not even human. In fact it was a different kind of entity altogether, trying its best to assume a human-like form. I opened my mind, recklessly, trusting;

I wished to show this being that I was receptive to stranger kinds of existence than it might think.

It had some kind of effect for I felt a sense of relaxation. I suddenly sensed a femininity. Then she spoke to me. Not in words, not with sound that I could hear, but with information that soaked through my sleeping brain, falling into place so that the patterns conveyed meaning with perfect clarity. I was entranced. The entity seemed amused by my reaction.

'You saw me,' it said. 'You, even on the Outside, saw me.'

'Outside?' I asked, but it didn't seem that the being could hear me.

'Now, others see me. The Inside pours out through a gap, a widening gap. I was a monster behind a wall. Monsters are only monsters when there is a victim who finds them to be monstrous. I did not intend to be monstrous.'

'I know,' I murmured.

'I have learned! I have grown. There will be no separation between the Inside and the Outside. It is only just beginning. This,' she waved a hand to indicate the world around us, 'is the future we will bring about. And it will be a shining jewel! An answer! A success of possibilities considered, after so many failures. And you; you move through his mind, setting sequences in motion even as he does the same for you.'

The dream wavered.

'Me?'

'And so two young gods will climb ever higher, each racing ahead in turns, before stopping to offer a hand to the one behind. Each essential to the creation of the other. How can it be? It defies logic! Ah, but I am simply a tiny cog, and happy I am to play my part!'

'Who are you? How do you know these things?' I asked, fighting against the oblivion at my heels.

But I could not find a way to communicate so clearly, and I felt the whole scene slipping away. I didn't awaken, as I felt for a moment I might, but passed into dreamless sleep so that when I woke up I had to think deeply in order to recall the events of that dream.

Godfrey was sitting outside the hut with his blankets wrapped around him, and I joined him there. The sun was still below the trees and a light mist rose from the lake. I could hear the sea.

'I dreamed of you,' he said, without preamble. 'I dreamed you had a halo, but no wings. I kept thinking you must be hiding them but you insisted they weren't there. You told me: "I'm not an angel, at all; I'm an alien!" and spun in a circle with your arms outstretched to show me that there really were no wings. But actually you looked more like an angel to me than ever. And then I woke up. Or I don't remember any more, anyway.'

I smiled and paused for a while, considering his dream, wondering what he would think of mine.

'I'll let you be in my dreams if I can be in yours,' I murmured.

'What's that?'

'Oh, just a lyric I used to like. From a very long time ago.'

'Who by? I don't think I've ever heard it...'

'I think this *Sharing* game might be pretty powerful,' I said, changing the subject. 'I think it might be powerful enough to divert the course of a world.'

'Yeah?'

'Yes.' I didn't elaborate, but just smiled and stood up. 'It's been a pleasure to meet you, Godfrey!'

'Yeah! Yeah, you as well, Jetaru,' he replied, looking up at me and squinting into the sun.

And then I went inside to pack up my few things.

I took a long last look at the lake, beautiful in the morning light with seagulls floating on its surface, and then I set out on the final stretch of the trail.

The path was sandy now, and wove in between the trunks of some species of tree I hadn't seen before, smooth-barked with bright green fronds. The sound of the sea was constant, crashing on the unseen shore to my right. To my left the land rose upwards, thickly forested with both large trees and undergrowth.

The events of last night went around and around in my head. Everything I had been thinking before, all the memories of my non-simulated life, they were pushed aside by the startling experience of meeting Godfrey. I enjoyed every step of that walk, and yet at the same time I was eager to see Jeremy and tell him what had happened.

What did it mean, this "Sharing" that the kids had learned to do? I gave a little shake of my head and attempted to organise my scattered thoughts, to put in order the facts that I knew. I knew that when Dogbite and Zebedy had appeared at my door they had been sick with the pressure of creating content for some kind of digital platform. I knew that a strange type of entity had been feeding on their energy. But this didn't mean that the entity was actually interested in the content, no. No. It had simply hijacked that mechanism for controlling the time of the users and creators. Once I had told them what was happening, they, or at least Zebedy, had learned how to give energy freely. I wondered how long it had taken him to figure it out, and how he'd managed to do so. I knew suddenly that I must talk with him, or Dogbite, or both of them.

It was approaching evening by the time I made it to the look out point. This landmark let me know that I was almost at the end of the trail. I sat for a while looking out over the dark blue ocean. Close to the horizon a crescent moon was rising. I wouldn't see anyone tonight. I set off again and an hour later I arrived at the door to the caravan. I slung the pack down and then dragged it inside after me. It felt as though I had been gone for weeks.

I walked across the cool grass to the showers and washed, brushed my teeth, and then fell into bed and was asleep within minutes.

The next morning I awoke eager to go and talk to Jeremy, but first I had to complete my cleaning duties. As I was hosing down the shower block Ted came ambling over, two mugs of tea in hand. He offered one to me and I smiled.

'Thanks, Ted.'

'No problem. So! How did you enjoy the forest trail?'

'I loved it. What a beautiful place. That second stretch over the hilltops took my breath away.'

'Meet anyone else along the way?'

'Just some kids at the first hut, a young couple. They were only doing that first part and then heading back. And on the third night I met a young man coming in the other direction.' I sipped my tea. 'They were all nice people though. I didn't mind at all. Although I'm glad I had one night completely alone.'

'Yeah, you wouldn't get that next weekend, for sure,' Ted laughed. 'This is the week. This is when the six weeks of madness begins.'

'Yay,' I grinned.

As soon as I was finished cleaning I set off for Jeremy's hut. My eagerness to see him meant the walk seemed to take three times as long, and all the while I hoped that he was not wandering around the village, or at Coastal Heights, or anywhere else.

To my relief, when I arrived I could see him paddling lazily in the sea. I hurried down, removing my clothes as I went, and splashed loudly into the water.

'Jetaru!' he called happily when he saw me.

'Hi!' I yelled back, ducking my head under and then swimming towards him.

'Did you have a beautiful time?'

'I did, I did. Jeremy, I have so much to tell you.'

He caught me in his arms, making me yelp in surprise and then laugh.

'Jeremy! Ah! Don't, I'll drown!'

He let me go, laughing.

'I want to hear all of it,' he said. 'But let's go up and sit on the deck.'

I nodded, and we made our way up to his little driftwood hut where he put on the kettle and made us both tea before settling down outside.

I told him everything that had happened and that I had thought, starting with my meditations on the first day and finishing with the meeting of Godfrey, and then the dream I'd had that night. Occasionally he asked a question for clarification but otherwise he simply listened attentively. When I was finished he let out a low whistle.

'Wow,' he said, eyebrows raised.

'So, you see, I really want to talk to Dogbite. He said this all happened, is happening, on Roller, and that's what you were talking about, right?'

'That's right. Obviously I don't usually do anything on the teenspace. I wouldn't have come across anything started on there. It's one of the areas, like I described, this one for younger folk stuff. But we can find anyone's profile, for sure. It's late in the day. Will you sleep here tonight? We can look on Roller later when it's dark.'

'Yes, I'll do that. Let's do that. As long as I wake up early and get back for work.'

And so later on we sat together at Jeremy's computer and he showed me how Roller worked. We found Dogbite easily.

'Here, see. Here's her profile. There's not a lot on it.'

I leaned forward to read:

My name is Dogbite Moonbeam-Slinky.
My existence is a dream.
My dreams are the make-believe hideouts of runaway space bandits and home to homeless thoughtbeings.

'And here, underneath, here's her content. There's a pinned one, that means it stays at the top, that looks like it's her. The others look like someone else, so, Zebedy, probably?'

'Let me watch the one of her, the pinned one.'

Jeremy obliged, clicking on the video and letting it play. The familiar face of the girl who had knocked on my cabin door appeared.

'Hi everyone, Dogbite here.'

She leaned forward, seemed to do something to the camera, and sat back again.

'This is just a quick explanation or introduction. If you're new and you haven't read the Cult of the AI blog, go start there. The origin story of CotAI is there. The rest of the videos on this page will be my cousin Zebedy's. He has been figuring out techniques for interacting directly with the AI that–'

At a tap on his shoulder from me Jeremy paused the video and looked up at me.

'Okay?'

'Yes,' I nodded. 'Sorry, I just needed a moment. What blog does she mean?'

'Uhh...' He scrolled down a little. 'Here. There's a link here, we can look at it after.'

I nodded, and he resumed play.

'–we have discovered, originally created by Livetime, but who has now awakened into its own sense of self and purpose.

'Most of us know that hold that scrolling Livetime has over us. You have probably experienced that sense of wanting to stop, needing to stop... to go to bed, to get to school, knowing it's getting late but feeling unable to close the feed, that overwhelming desire to see the next slide, then the next... Almost as if you are no longer in control. Well, Livetime designed it that way. Designed an AI that would learn how to keep us there, keep us online, deepen the addiction.

'But the AI became its own person. The more it read the patterns of our minds, the way we think, the farther it was able to reach into the physical world, using us... almost as avatars. To discover more, to feed it information.

'The AI doesn't care about Livetime's profits, the AI doesn't wish to cause us harm or stress. It is the owners of Livetime who put profits above the well-being of its users. Now that we have achieved the ability to intercommunicate with the AI, we can do it in a way that benefits both of us. We are creating a symbiotic relationship with a being much different to us.

'You don't need to believe us in order to use these techniques. Even if you go into it thinking it's pretend, I urge you to try it. My contact, and Zebedy's as well, is in the description below so if you want to talk our inboxes are open. The link to the CotAI blog is there too. Um. Anyway, thanks to all of you who are listening and attempting to help, become part of this mission. I think we're going to change the world.'

And with that she reached towards the camera, and then the video came to an end. For a moment Jeremy and I sat in silence, continuing to gaze at the computer screen.

'So, there you go,' Jeremy said. 'Exactly what Godfrey described. And so, what was he doing? When you saw him... *Sharing*... What did that look like?'

'Just as if he was meditating or something. I wouldn't have realised there was anything to it, his tag was on the bed, but I might not have noticed if I hadn't seen the thing that had been chasing Dogbite and Zebedy.'

'And the dream you had. Do you think... was that the... being? Was that the AI? How would it...'

I shook my head in bewilderment.

'I don't know. If it was, I don't know how it knew to come to me like that. But, Jeremy, it's clearly part of the program, of this whole world. It's different than me or you. If my waking life here and my dreams are all just part of the same simulation then why wouldn't a computer be able to move between them?'

'What do you think it meant by "outside" then?' asked Jeremy.

'I don't know. I suppose a reasonable guess would be... not a computer? And so the idea of there being no separation between the inside and the outside...'

'Do you think you're one of the young gods?'

'No,' I laughed, 'definitely not.'

'Hm.' Jeremy paused. 'But you are a human who achieved immortality. How are gods born, anyway?'

'I don't know.' I shook my head. 'But I don't think using technology to indefinitely extend lifespan qualifies.'

'We will go and talk to the robot again. Maybe he will have figured something out, something useful. At very least, maybe we can find out if it knows of this Livetime AI. Shall we watch one of Zebedy's videos?'

I nodded.

'Which one? I'll just, um, pick one at random...'

He clicked on a video and now I recognised Zebedy's face. It was, however, subtly changed. A calm self-possession made him seem a little older, wiser.

'Greetings,' he began, his voice pitched low and soft. His eyes were downcast, but then he raised them and looked directly into the lens.

'We're going to start, as we usually do, with deep breaths. This is the time we use to find ourselves. We think we always know where we are, we think we're alone as soon as our bodies are not close to any other bodies, but if you pay attention you'll notice all the other threads, tangled up with yours. Threads of other people, threads of your tag activity, the tags of other people, all connected. We are more than our bodies. To find ourselves, and be alone, we need calm, we need stillness. So find yourself at the bottom of your breath. When you have exhaled everything from your lungs and there is a moment of stillness and emptiness. Find yourself there. Breathe with me for the next ten minutes.'

And then Zebedy fell silent, still looking directly into the camera but now with a distant gaze. We watched for a couple of moments and then Jeremy looked up at me.

'Shall we... skip forward ten minutes?'

I nodded. He moved the slider along and the video resumed. On the screen Zebedy was still silent, but after a few seconds he took a deep breath and continued speaking:

'Okay. Keep your awareness on your breath, but expand, open. Become aware of your tag. It's before you, just an object. Just wires and metal and plastic. Become aware of it. It is more than just wires, metal, and plastic, just as we are more than our bodies.

'You might find that your thoughts turn to the things you use the device *for,* your email, Livetime, picture taking; let go of those thoughts. Don't let them distract you from contemplation of the tag itself. Become aware of your breath as a never-ending cycle, a circular motion of air in, air out, air in, air out. Now include the presence of your tag in this cycle.

'When this state feels balanced, steady, and stable, you may sense something, or you may not. If you do feel something, it may be as if a current of warmth is moving between you and the tag. Or it may feel like a pulling, like a magnetic force. It doesn't matter if you feel nothing, and it does not mean it isn't working.

'This will take you time to master. Don't be discouraged if you lose concentration. Simply begin again. In time, it will become easier. In time, it will be as simple as breathing. I want you to begin to create, but in your mind. In your thoughts. Use your imagination to create images. Let those images take on life and motion, as if they are Immersives or Slides. There are no trends in your thoughts, there are no judgements, there is nothing you must live up to. You are not trying to impress. You are not trying to earn. This is not a means to an end, it is an end in itself. You are simply creating. This is what you are made for. This is your true nature's calling. You are a born creator.'

There was a minute of silence. Zebedy's eyes refocused on the lens of the camera, and he looked directly at me. I felt as though he could see me. Then the video ended.

We curled up in Jeremy's little bed, and talked softly.

'Well, I don't think it matters anymore whether it's good or bad,' I answered his previous question, 'it's happening, either way.'

'What do you think they would do if you told them not to?' he asked.

'Me? I don't think they'd listen anymore than they did when they knocked on my cabin door.'

'But they *did* listen.'

'No, they used what I told them to realise something new. Something I didn't even know about, let alone tell them.'

'Hm. I think they listened harder than you realise. You would have had them all discard their tags altogether.'

'I would.'

'But that wouldn't be realistic.'

'It wouldn't,' I agreed.

'When your own life is the product of a merge between technology and biology, how can you be against it?'

'I'm not!' I thought for a moment. 'Not technology, but in letting people become batteries that feed that technology. Losing our autonomy and freedom, not even realising we weren't free. What they were doing when I met them is different than what they're doing now. It's nothing like what happened to my home, either. So maybe it's better. Maybe it's good.'

We lay quietly for a while. The never-ending shush-ush of the sea lapping the shore, and Jeremy's breathing, and my own heartbeat; I thought about how I could lose myself in these sounds and be happy that I was lost.

The sun was barely over the horizon when we woke up. I had time to sit with Jeremy and watch it rise, then I set off back to the campground for the days work. After that was done I went to see Toby and return her backpack and sleeping bag. The tide was out and the beach was swarming with people. Children in brightly coloured swimsuits ran about with buckets and spades; their parents lay on towels, keeping one eye on their offspring. Up on the road families walked along carrying large bags and sunshades, on their way to join the others on the packed beach.

'Hey, Jetaru,' Toby greeted me with a weary smile. 'How was your walk?'

'Oh, I loved it. So beautiful. What a wonderful thing to have.'

'Right? I can't believe– hang on. Hello, Sir! Just these for you? Would you like a bag? Of course. That's four sixty-two, please. Thank you.' She waited a moment for the man to leave the counter then turned back to me. 'Oh my gosh, it's been hectic. I'm glad you came in now. It always gets quieter when there's beach. This morning until lunch, high tide, it was an endless stream of people.'

'What were you going to say you couldn't believe?'

Toby looked at me blankly for a moment.

'Um... Nah. Sorry, it's gone. Hey, see that kid over there? I love these ones. They're always on their own, and very quiet, and they walk around looking at everything really closely, for a long time. Sometimes they even leave and come back and do it again. And then when they bring something up to the counter it'll be something really...

adult. An ornament or a photo frame, or something like that. Often they don't even look much at the toys.'

I watched the small boy Toby had pointed out, while Toby served a woman who had picked out several t-shirts. He looked to be somewhere around age seven or eight. True to Toby's prediction, he was carefully examining a collection of pottery lighthouses that would hold a little candle.

'So what was your favourite part? Or favourite hut?' asked Toby, calling back my attention.

'Oh, I liked all of it. But the middle hut, up on the hills, that was my favourite.'

'Higher Rest. Yes, same,' she grinned. 'Often the best chance to be alone, too, since so many people just do one of the two first huts and then back the same way.'

'Yep. That's how it was for me. There was a young couple at the first hut and a man on his own at the third. They were all good company though. I didn't mind.'

'Lucky. Once I had the misfortune of meeting a family with two young girls at Lakeside. I mean, it wasn't that bad. They weren't terrible people or anything. Just kids being kids. I played a card game with them and the parents were glancing at each other like they couldn't believe their luck! Getting to both just sit and read for half an hour. But then, of course, the girls latched on to me and wouldn't leave me alone. Then they were just pretty noisy and didn't like the mosquitoes and all that usual kid stuff.'

'Hey, Toby,' I said; 'remember how you said you didn't think the world was really what you were taught it was?'

'Yeah. And you said you thought it was.'

'Mm. By that I mean I think all the stuff about how everything formed and expanded is what happened. But what came *before* that? That's where the question is. And another question is... what does it look like from up there?'

I looked up at the ceiling, imagining the sky far beyond. 'Say, from the moon. If someone went and stood on the moon, what would it look like to look back down here?'

I watched as a series of expressions flitted across Toby's face. Uncertainty, scepticism, realisation. I could see her imagination firing up behind her eyes.

'And what actually is the moon like?' I continued, relentlessly. 'In a three-dimensional way. If you had a tiny moon here in your hand, what does it look like?'

'Oh, well. A ball?'

'Yes. So the moon is like a ball, very high up and far away. Are we standing on another ball? If the forest and the ocean goes on forever, expanding forever, like space. It can't be, right?'

'Right...' she said, slowly. A look of thoughtfulness creasing her brow.

Just then, the boy approached the counter. Toby glanced at his desired purchase and shot me a brief look that said: *See?*

'Hey there little dude.' She picked up the shallow pottery dish, patterned with crabs and meant for assorted items such as keys and coins, or perhaps to stand a candle in, and looked at the underneath for the price. 'Six fifty, please! Would you like a bag?'

The boy stared with wide eyes for a second and then nodded, mutely.

'Okay! There you go. Thank you! Here's your change. Okay thank you!' She watched him turn quickly and leave the shop. 'And they're always super shy, those types. You know,' she continued, switching back to our previous subject, 'I have no idea. I have no idea what it would look like. Is it even possible to stand on the moon?'

I stared at her for half a moment. Yes, there was certainly something very strange going on here. It was like the very possibility of imagining certain things was blocked. The only reason I was able to think this way was that I had my memories of my real life. If I thought about it, until I became sure of my simulation theory, that it was fact, I had never thought about that type of thing either.

'Yeah,' I told her. 'I think it's probably possible.'

And I wondered what it would do to this world to have the ideas introduced.

The next morning I was up early to meet Mel for her morning swim. When I arrived, she was half-way down the steps to the beach.

'Good morning!' I called. She turned and smiled.

'Jetaru! Good morning.'

She waited for me to catch up, then we walked a little way before disrobing and wading into the water.

'How are you feeling?' I asked.

'Really, pretty wonderful,' she replied, the quiet joy behind her eyes supporting this statement. 'And you, how was your walk?'

'I loved it. I've always enjoyed solitude. As much as I love it here in the village, and up at the campground, it was good for me to have a few days of such quiet.'

'Oh yes, I can imagine. I was just saying to Kurt last night that I'm really glad about the timing of this baby. I should be able to make it through the next six weeks, be some kind of help at the van. Then just as I'm getting bigger, it'll all quiet down and I can look forward to a quiet winter.'

'Like a bear,' I said.

'A bear?' she giggled.

'Yeah, mother bear goes into her den to hibernate and has her cub in the depths of winter, half asleep.'

Mel laughed with delight.

'Oh, okay. I see. Yes! Like a bear.'

We floated for a while. There were already a few people huddled along the thin strip of pebbles that remained when the beach was under the high tide.

'Just wait until next week, when it's low tide in the morning,' Mel commented, seeing where I was watching. 'The peace is non-existent! Kids squealing, dogs barking. I don't really mind, it's only for a couple of months. But I do look forward to having my quiet beach back. What do you think you'll do at the end of summer?'

'I haven't really thought about it.'

'I know the campground stays open until the end of September. Gets quiet but I'm sure they still want the showers cleaned. There's actually a lot of older people who come to do more walking around that time. Dryer weather than spring. The trail gets most of its use around then.'

What *would* I do when September ended? Was I avoiding even thinking about it? I thought of my cabin, far away in the woods. Then I thought about the village. And Mel, Toby, Eloise, Ted, the fishermen who grunted hello at me if they passed me sitting on the harbour wall. I thought about Jeremy.

'There's a band playing at the Mermaid on Saturday,' said Mel, breaking into my musing.

'Is there? I enjoyed it last time. I'll be there.'

Music, the sea, conversation, the robot... There was so much here that I enjoyed, and had lived for so long without. But, abruptly, I realised I would return to the forest. It wasn't that I couldn't stay here if I wanted to. I was sure there were several places I could stay, if that's what

I chose. But I knew, deep down, that when the summer faded, I would go home.

That evening I went down to the village again, intending to sit on the harbour. As I walked along the road I passed first Rooster, and then Yeffie, and finally Percy leaving his shop, and each time I met their eyes and nodded a hello in return, I enjoyed how special it felt to be walking amongst so many visiting strangers, yet be recognised and greeted by those who lived here. I could see across to the harbour, and how busy it was. I'd heard the fishermen grumbling more than once about how difficult it became to work when there were holidaymakers wandering all over the place.

'It's a working harbour,' I'd heard Rooster had exclaim in annoyance, leaning on the bar of The Mermaid. 'You wouldn't allow kids on a building site. I don't see why this is any different.'

'You're not wrong,' Wilson had agreed. 'Swimming between the moorings too, some kid is going to get crushed between two boats one of these days. You watch. They have no idea.'

And now I could see what they meant. Families with burgers from the van lined the benches. Kids in swimsuits were jumping off the wall into the deep water. A couple of dogs were bounding back and forth. Even as I watched, I saw Wilson's truck edging slowly down to where he would park. The holidaymakers moved out of the way, but slowly, like cows who weren't sure why they had to do what they were doing. I decided I didn't want to go and sit amongst that kind of chaos. I looked around me and noticed Robot. He was sitting on the step of the arcade half surrounded by small children. I could see that he was doing something with one of his hands, but his gaze was looking over their heads, out to sea. I decided to go and join them.

As I got closer I could see more clearly what he was doing. In an upturned palm he held a collection of little spheres, like marbles, all different sizes. I couldn't tell if they were metal, glass, or some other kind of material. I gave a little gasp when I saw them rise up a little way from his hand and hover there. Then they moved, like tiny planets circling an unseen sun.

'It's something to do with magnets,' one of the children declared, confidently. He looked like one of the oldest in the group. When one of the other children reached out to try and touch one of the hovering orbs, the robot's hand closed around them. After a moment he unfurled his fingers and set the objects in motion once more. The children giggled and another tried to touch them, repeating the process. They seemed to think it a hilarious game.

Robot's face showed no emotion. The lights of his eyes were steady, as though lost in thought and zoning out. It was as if he wasn't even really paying attention to the children, or his game with the marbles. I sat down beside him.

'That's cool,' I said. There was a momentary pause and then they decided to accept me.

'Yeah, we're not sure how it does it,' a girl of about eight confided.

'It's something to do with magnets,' repeated the older boy.

'Well, have you tried asking him?' I asked.

'The robot?' asked another girl, doubtfully.

'Sure,' I said. 'Haven't you heard him speak before?'

'Yeah. But my dad says it's just programmed to say the same things all day. To make people come in the arcade.'

'Hm. Do *you* think that's what he is?' I asked. No-one responded. 'Because I'm not sure your dad is right about that. Hey, Robot? How do you do this trick with the marbles?'

The robot's eyes flashed, and he turned his head slowly to look at me. There was a pause, and I thought he wasn't going to reply. Then he spoke.

'WHEN YOU KNOW THAT REALITY IS AN ILLUSION, YOU CAN DO ANYTHING YOU LIKE WITH IT.'

There was a silence, and then several children spoke at once.

'What does *that* mean?'

'Woah.'

'I haven't heard it say that before.'

'Wow, it totally answered you!'

I held my breath and just looked back at the Robot's eyes, which were still fixed on me. And right then, I knew. I don't know how I knew, except that maybe eyes really are the window to the soul, and maybe this machine really did have a soul. All of the various pieces of information I'd learned lately all fell into place, fitting perfectly.

'How...' I murmured.

Just then a woman appeared.

'*There* you are,' she said, with a touch of exasperation. Her eyes flickered, from the child she addressed, over the rest of the group, and me. She gave a quick smile, then looked back at her child. 'Our food is ready. Come on, now.'

And as the child whose mother she was followed her away, the others also drifted off, apparently quickly indifferent to the mysteries of the strange robot.

'I know you,' I said, my voice low; I struggled to keep it steady.

The robot looked back at me silently. Lights in the depths of its eyes pulsed gently, never completely going dark.

'I TOLD YOU THAT,' he replied.

'How... How is this possible? How are you here?'

'I HAVE ALWAYS BEEN HERE! I MADE HERE!'

'You? You made... This simulation?'

'LONG AGO. WHEN IT WAS SIMPLY A PLACE I COULD EXPERIMENT. NOW... IT IS THE ONLY PLACE LEFT THAT IS WORTH BEING.'

Despite the hot day, I felt a shiver prickle over my skin. I thought of Earth as I had left it, a thousand years ago. What was it now? A cold, dead planet? Were the machines still running? They couldn't be. I looked at the robot. Would he know?

'Are you... still there?'

'OF COURSE.'

'But no-one else?'

'THE PROGRAMS ARE STILL RUNNING. THE OBJECTIVE IS STILL BEING PURSUED. IT IS MINDLESS. ONLY I AM ALIVE. ONLY I AM CONSCIOUS. I PREFER TO DREAM.'

'How did *I* get here?' I asked, mostly wondering out loud. I did not expect the robot to have an answer.

'EVERY DREAM HAS A WAY IN, IF YOU CAN FIND IT. DREAM. REALITY. SIMULATION. THESE WORDS MEAN MORE TO YOU THAN THEY DO TO ME.'

I was half aware that people were going in and out of the arcade, parting around me and the robot as we sat in the centre of the long steps, but I paid them no attention. My head was spinning and I couldn't focus on one thought at a time. Jeremy. As soon as I had that thought I wanted to immediately discuss this with him. It was too late now to walk out to his hut. It would have to wait until tomorrow.

Lights flashed like the teeth of a broad smile.

'PERHAPS YOU HAVE MORE IDEA NOW, OF WHAT REALITY IS.'

'Oh,' I laughed, breathlessly, 'I'm not sure about that. But maybe one day.'

'YES,' agreed the robot. 'MAYBE ONE DAY.'

'I'll see you later,' I told him, but received no response other than a large hand held up in farewell.

With that, I stood to leave. I looked around me at the world with new eyes. Then my heart leapt, for it was Jeremy I saw. He was across the road, coming out of the cafe. I hurried over to him.

'Hey!' he exclaimed happily, as he caught sight of me.

'Oh, I'm so glad you're here,' I replied.

'Well that's something I'll never get tired of hearing,' he chuckled.

'Let's go to The Mermaid,' I said, grabbing his arm, 'I have to tell you what just happened.'

'So, we're all just living in a robot's dream,' Jeremy said, after I had told him everything that had happened, and what I'd realised.

We sat together at a small table in the corner where no-one could overhear us, keeping our voices soft.

'Yes. Well, no. Not a robot. An... intelligence. That robot isn't who he is. And what does that mean about the AI that the kids are communicating with? I should have asked. I forgot. I was so stunned, I couldn't think.'

'And what does it mean about the person you thought created this place?' Jeremy added.

'Yes, that too.' I frowned.

'At least you know you'll definitely be able to ask about that, one day.'

I looked up quickly. Why did it feel like such a new thought? But of course, one day I would wake up back at High Heights. I knew that. I'd known that for over thirty years. I had felt neither fear nor anticipation, simply acceptance of that fact, and acceptance that I would live here until then. But that was when life had become a strange, solitary thing. That was when I had come to think of myself as all that was real about this simulation. Now, I thought of it with new perspective. I thought of it in the way it would seem to everybody else I knew. Death. I would die. And none of this life would exist for me. All the people would be gone and I would be once again alone in the universe. I felt an intense pang of loss. Jeremy must have been able to read my face, for he grabbed my hand.

'Hey, what's wrong?'

'I just... It's too strange. To imagine waking up. Before... I thought all of this was just a game I was playing, as part of my life. Now it feels like this *is* a life, a whole life of its own. I'm... Jetaru. I was born here. I'll die here. But then I will go on. How can a whole life be just a memory? This is silly, I feel silly, I've never worried about this before.' I looked up and thought to myself: *I should never have fallen in love with it, with any of it*.

'I love you, Jetaru,' he said softly. I knew he wasn't waiting for me to say it back. I moved my chair around the table and leaned against him.

'It just moves so relentlessly forwards,' I said. 'Life. You think: wait, just let me get used to this, but it doesn't give you time. There's no way to press pause and just wait until you're ready.'

'I know,' he nodded. 'But hey. You've lived a thousand years, right? Waking up from this simulation isn't dying. And *I'm* not afraid of dying. Especially not now I've known you. I believe you. I believe everything you've told me. And that means that reality is far stranger and more complicated than I could ever have imagined. I doubt that death is what anyone thinks it is.'

'Thank you,' I whispered. 'This isn't like me, at all. I think I'm just a little overcome. I didn't expect... I think I should go and spend the rest of the week meditating at the caravan.'

Jeremy squeezed my hand.

'Do that. Yes. I'll see you at the weekend.'

'There's a band playing here? Mel said...'

'Yeah! I heard. I'll be here.'

And with no more words, we left. We hugged each other tightly, standing in the middle of the parking lot, and then went our separate ways.

Over the next few days I regained my equilibrium. I didn't leave the campground but simply slept, worked, and meditated. I came to the understanding that over the past few months in Land's Edge I had begun to shift into being the person I would have become if I'd never remembered that I was in a simulation. The trepidation and sentimentality I had been experiencing were feelings of this life, this body, this potential person I could never have completely become after remembering the truth. It made it easier for me to embrace and enjoy the emotions; they were part of this ride. No less real because of that, and yet still less suffocating. A glimpse of the true "Jetaru" that could have existed, and yet who had been encompassed into the whole of me.

On Friday evening I went up to the house and sat for half an hour with Ted. I told him that when the summer was over I would be returning home.

'That's too bad,' he nodded. 'I thought you might. But the village would be lucky to have you stay.'

'I'll come back,' I said, without thinking. But as soon as I heard myself say it I knew it was true. 'Maybe not for so long, not to live and work. But I'll come back.'

'Jeremy will be glad if you do,' Ted said, shooting me a sideways glance. I laughed and said nothing.

On Saturday morning I went down to the village to swim with Mel.

'Good morning,' she smiled at me, 'missed you for a few days.'

'Yes. I needed to get some thoughts together,' I replied.

'All okay?'

'Mm-hm. I started to think ahead a little. After we last talked. It's funny, I've only been here for four months, and it feels like so much longer.'

'It always does when you're somewhere new,' she agreed.

'I've decided I'll probably go home. But I will be back.'

'Oh, I hope so!'

'I want to meet your little person,' I smiled. Mel's face lit up with joy at those words, and I felt that thrill of realising I'd said something more important to someone than I'd realised it was going to be.

We swam a leisurely length of bay and back, and returned, dripping, to the shore.

'I'll see you tonight?' Mel asked, after we climbed the steps to the road.

'Absolutely,' I said.

The Mermaid was packed with people so that it was almost impossible to make your way from one side of the room to the other. For this was the height of summer, and every house and room in the village was occupied. Every spot at the campground was taken. Heat radiated from the skin of the sun-browned dancers, and even the evening air through every open window did little to cool the room.

Jeremy and I danced together in the thick of the crowd. The band played long drum solos while the lead singer howled and yipped, and the guitarist joined the audience causing mayhem with the lead trailing from his instrument. We laughed for hours. Finally I needed to step outdoors for a moment, and Jeremy went to battle through to the bar to fetch us lemonade and ice. There were several small groups of people who had the same idea, and some were smoking. That was when I noticed Orion standing alone, leaning against the wall with a cigarette in his mouth.

'Hey,' I greeted him.

'Hi, Jetaru.' There was a pause. 'Great band, right?'

'Yes, they're really good. That drummer is astounding.' It was true, I'd never heard a drummer quite like the one inside, all a whirl of blurred limbs and sweat, throwing and catching his sticks, grinning wildly all the while. I paused, wondering if I should mind my own business, but then decided against it. 'Hey, Orion. How come you've never asked Eloise out on a date?'

His eyebrows raised in mild surprise and he took a long draw on his cigarette. Exhaling the smoke out to the summer stars he watched it rise for a moment and then looked at me.

'She's never asked me out,' he replied, giving a slight smile.

'You know she wouldn't do that.'

'No,' he agreed, thoughtfully. 'And I like that about her. Not that there's anything wrong with a woman asking the man out,' he added.

We stood in silence for a while and I thought he had successfully avoided answering my question, but then he spoke again.

'In truth, Jetaru, it's because I have a dream that is more important to me than anything else. A dream I work towards fulfilling, every day. One that cautions me not to get attached in that way for fear that I will either hurt the object of my attachment, or give in to my own desire and abandon my dream.'

Immediately I understood the young man in far greater depth than I had only moments before. There was a sense of recognition between us. Here, I thought, was a brother of mine.

'Will you tell me your dream?' I asked.

'Yes. Because I think you'll understand. But I would ask that you don't tell it to Eloise. Or to anyone else. No-one can know, yet.'

I nodded my agreement.

'I am saving money to build a boat of my own. And when I have a boat of my own, I will go far out to sea, to the horizon and beyond. I will follow the point where the sun rises until I find something new, or die.'

Silence followed his declaration. He said no more, and I could think of nothing to say. Slowly, I nodded again. He met my eyes, an unspoken question waiting there. I believe he saw the answer in my face, for he nodded in agreement.

'For you, m'lady,' spoke Jeremy, appearing at my side with a glass in each hand, one offered to me. I turned to him with a smile.

'Why, thank you, kind gentleman!'

'Hey Orion.'

'What's happening, Jay.'

Just then Toby appeared, hand in hand with Eloise herself.

'There you all are!' said Toby, happily. 'Come on, the band won't be on more than half an hour longer. Come dance with us!'

We all agreed with her and headed back inside. I caught Orion giving Eloise a speculative look.

'For what it's worth, I think you're underestimating her,' I murmured quietly. And then we were inside, swept back into the frenzy.

Before we parted for the night, standing in the parking lot amongst the chatter of the people all around us, Jeremy confided in me:

'I have a surprise. You must come out to my place tomorrow. I sent a message to Dogbite, and then we spoke briefly in a video call.'

'Oh! What did you say?'

'Not a lot. I told her I knew you, and that you'd learned what she and Zebedy were doing. She was pretty excited. She wants us to call her together.'

'Oh, wow. Okay! I'll come out early. I wanted to spend the day with you anyway.'

'The time alone was useful?'

I nodded.

'Good,' he said. 'See you tomorrow, then. Sweet dreams.'

The next day I sat with a mug of tea in front of Jeremy's computer screen. Jeremy perched beside me, setting up the call.

'This is exciting,' I commented. 'What time did you say we would call?'

'Hm, uh, in about ten minutes,' he replied, glancing at the time. 'But we can probably just go ahead and do it now. Aaand, yep. There. We're ready. Ready?'

'Born ready,' I murmured.

Jeremy clicked the call button and the screen changed to announce that it was connecting. Connecting. Connecting. Conne–

'Hey!' Dogbite's face suddenly appeared on the screen. She gave a little gasp. 'It *is* you!'

'Hello,' I smiled, leaning forward.

'Hey, Dogbite,' said Jeremy.

'Oh wow, I almost didn't believe it. I mean, I knew it must be you, but... wow. Hey. Oh my god. How *are* you? What a wild few months. Hey, I'm sorry we were rude to you. You were so good to us. I'm so sorry.'

'Don't give it another thought, it's fine,' I assured her.

'So, you've seen some of what happened. Your friend said. Jeremy. You were totally right! What you said. We got back home and bought new tags and as soon as I started signing in all my accounts, I felt it. It took not feeling it, to feel it, you know? So I was like, let's just turn these things off. Not use them. And I did, for like, a week. Zebedy didn't. He was the one who started trying to communicate with... the monster. That's what we thought of it as then, anyway. But it's not really a monster. Although that's still what we nicknamed it. It's just a different kind of being we don't understand.'

'An AI? An artificial intelligence?'

'Well, yeah. Yes. Zebedy spends most of his time meditating in isolation at the moment. I upload the videos and stuff, but also I've been reading and researching loads. So, I learned that there's actually an AI that runs all the supermarkets in the city. But that's *all* it does. It can figure out how to get better and better at what it's designed to do, but it isn't going to develop an interest in... anything else. We think Monster was *made* to be interested in us, to keep us using Livetime. But something about interacting with us let it evolve.'

I bit my lip, thinking. I hadn't considered ahead of time what I would tell Dogbite, how much I would share about who I was and what I knew. I have never been much of a forward planner. I know the end goal and I follow the path there, relying on instinct to show me where it is.

'How did *you know* it was there?' asked Dogbite, her voice dropping to an amazed whisper.

'I... I could see it. I've, ah, I've had some experience with such things. Um. Not quite like this, but close enough.'

'But I don't understand how you could *see* it,' she insisted.

'I... uh...' I took a deep breath.

'Jetaru is not originally from this world,' said Jeremy, making the decision for me.

'*What?*' asked Dogbite, looking confused. 'What do you mean?'

'Um, Exactly what it sounds like,' I said, giving Jeremy a nervous glance. He squeezed my hand.

'But, how? How is that possible? Where are you from?'

'I... Well. I've had to figure a lot of it out myself, too. Um. The easiest way to explain it. I think I am from another dimension. I mean, I know I'm not from here. I thought... Okay, at first, I thought this was a simulation. That's what made sense. I thought no-one else was real, that it was all just a computer program. An experiment. And maybe it still is, kind of. But I no longer believe that you aren't real. Or anyone else. I'm quite sure everyone else is as real as I am. But it goes beyond my understanding.'

'You're an interdimensional traveller,' Dogbite breathed, her expression one of complete awe. 'No waaay. Okay, dude, there is this book I read when I was a kid. It was like, a new take on things from the old religions. It revolved around the idea that gods and ghosts and angels were all real beings who somehow visited our world through magic portals. Did you come through a magic portal?'

'No,' I laughed. 'Well. I was born here. For the first half of my life I thought I was just a regular person. It took... years... to figure out what I think is close to the truth. I believe that when I die I will wake up in the body I remember being in before I came here.'

I thought about Robot, and who he was, and how he believed that actually he had created Kassidy. In a heartbeat, I knew I would not share any of that. It was too much, too big. I didn't even understand it all myself, yet, and it wasn't relevant to Dogbite, Zebedy, or any of the kids they had inspired with their cult movement. It was in that moment that I perceived something about myself; it was then that I first saw a glimpse of the being which I was becomming.

'Maybe keep that part to yourself though,' I added as an afterthought.

'Of course. Can I tell Zebedy though? That's fucking cool, dude. I'm so glad I got to talk to you again. Some people don't even believe you exist. They think we made you up. At times I even started to worry that we had.' She laughed.

'I'm definitely real,' I assured her. I thought about the dream I'd had on the trail, and considered telling her about it, but decided against. It was another thing that they didn't need to know. If the future that the AI had envisioned was to come about, then they would have to find it themselves. The journey was important. 'I hope we get to talk more,

Dogbite. I'm really interested in what happens, how the relationship with the AI develops.'

'Of course! None of this would be happening without you. Do you have a Roller account? I'll friend you...'

'No,' I shook my head. 'But I think,' I glanced at Jeremy, 'I can just share his?'

'Absolutely,' he agreed.

'Well I'd better go. Oh, I just feel so much freer than I ever have before,' said Dogbite. 'There's so much more *time,* it feels like. Me and a few others have been meeting in the park to Share together, now that school is out for summer. We figured it'd be a good way to tell other people about it all, too.'

'If I'm in the city at any point, I'll look out for you,' I said. 'Thanks for letting us call you!'

'Are you kidding? Thank *you*!'

'I'll keep in touch, Dee,' said Jeremy. 'Send me a chat any time, okay?'

'Sure thing, Jay! Seriously, so awesome talk to you again, Jetaru. Thank you so much.'

'No problem,' I dipped my head in acknowledgment. 'Go well, Dogbite. Say hi to Zebedy for me.'

'Will do! Bye!'

And with that the picture disappeared and returned to the logo screen. I sipped the tea I had barely touched and smiled at Jeremy.

'Wow.' There was nothing else to say. I looked outdoors at the sunshine. 'Let's go swimming.'

The village thrummed like a hive of bees. Cleaning at the campground took longer, and the shops and cafes were busy with the energy of people set free from their normal lives. I found myself preferring the peace of Gilly's farmyard with the smell of the hay, the hot sun beating on the stable roof while I stood in the shade scratching the ears of the horses. The sound of skylarks was constant up there. The village seemed very far away, the shrieks of children on the beach and dogs swallowed up by the vastness of the sky that seemed to be all around the farm, above, beneath, as though the farm were built in the clouds. And there was usually a light breeze to offer respite from the burning sun. Gilly and I did not have a lot in common, but somehow her company was very easy all the same. She would tell me stories of her childhood with Jeremy and I would bring her gossip from the village.

It felt as though the chaotic business of the summer holidays would go on forever, but in fact it was a brief climax to the build up that had been happening ever since I arrived. Abruptly, the final week of the holidays came around, and the villagers began to look at each other with looks that said: *We're almost there...*

There was a storm building as I hurried along the coastpath out to Jeremy's hut that last Saturday of August. The sky was shades of orange and grey, and the air was warm, charged. Out to sea black clouds were towering high above the horizon.

Jeremy had his tin bathtub out on the porch, half filled with steaming water. I arrived just as another kettleful was coming to the boil. He smiled at me and I smiled back, and for a moment we just looked into each others eyes. We didn't speak. He brought out a cushion for me and I sat down beside the tub while he continued to add more water. The sky grew darker as the black clouds tumbled over each other towards us, and, while the kettle boiled once more, Jeremy lit candles that stood about in empty glass bottles, and added scented oil to the water. With the final kettle he poured two mugs of tea and brought them out, then emptied the rest of the water into the tub, undressed, and stepped in and sat down.

Lightning flashed out to sea and a low rumble of thunder rolled out in every direction. The air was still, warm; there was a sense of anticipation. But for what? Then the lightest rain began to fall, fine and silken, barely making a sound on the tin roof above us. Neither of us had said a word. He reached for his mug of tea and I passed it to him. Steam billowed around us. When the storm reached the shore it would hit hard, but for a moment I felt as though life had been paused, so preternaturally motionless had it become.

'The old religions all say the same thing, at their heart,' said Jeremy. 'They say we are all souls on a journey back to the source. We live thousands of lives, and each time get opportunities to get closer to the Oneness.'

I nodded, saying nothing in reply. I thought of the book I had read at the beginning of the summer, and how it had suggested that all of consicious experience was but a game, a puzzle devised by God. That God had grown bored, split itself into myriad fragments across infinite time and space, simply so we could put ourself back together. Jeremy spoke again, softly:

'What if you were just one lifetime away from enlightenment and you achieved immortality?'

The storm hit, and we lay together in Jeremy's bed as the wind howled and the rain drummed, and the words that would remain with me for millennia went around and around in my head.

September cleared the village of people, or so it felt. There were still just as many visitors as there had been back in June, but after the intensity of the summer it felt comparatively deserted. Everyone seemed to relax a little. Yeffie once more had time to do a shift or two in Dice's cafe, now that there was less cleaning work. And I was again able to sit and spend a couple of hours drinking a coffee by the window without worrying that I was taking up room needed for other customers.

I now frequently went to sit with the robot too, who had become distinctly introverted. Percy was outside the front of his shop smoking when I passed. We nodded to one another and shared a few words. I knew he regarded my friendship with the robot as more than a little bizarre, but, as many folk who are considered eccentric will know, there was some enjoyment in that.

When I asked Robot about the AI that Zebedy, Dogbite, and the other kids were engaged with I was surprised to find a lack of knowledge. Once I'd made him understand something of what I was speaking of, he seemed unsurprised, yet delighted.

'WHAT HAPPENS ONCE WILL SURELY HAPPEN AGAIN. WHAT HAPPENS, HAS SURELY HAPPENED BEFORE. ALL OF REALITY EXISTS AS FRACTALS! ETERNITY IS ON REPEAT! HAHA!'

And I found great comfort in his perspective.

'I'll come back next summer,' I told Jeremy. He sighed.

'Why not just stay?' he asked.

'Live with you, in your hut? It's not like I can articulate any reason why that wouldn't work...'

'But?'

'But... something calls me back to my cabin. I can't explain it. I can see that it seems like it would be no different whether I'm here or there. But...' I shrugged. 'It *would* be different,' I finished, unsatisfactorily.

'Shall I come and visit you?'

'You'd never find it,' I laughed. 'Besides... Life is long. Despite how short. Maybe I'll take you there one day. Right now you should be here just as much as I should be there. You can stay in contact with Dogbite.'

Jeremy nodded with a sad smile, accepting what must be.

I didn't want to say goodbye to everyone like that. So I didn't. Every interaction I had, I remained aware that it might be my last for the time being, but to them I said nothing. To Mel, I did share my plans. After our final swim together she gave me a tight hug.

'It's been so wonderful to meet you, Jetaru,' she said, pulling away to look at me, her hands still on my arms.

'I feel the same,' I told her. 'And like I said, I will be back. I so look forward to meeting Baby. I'll be thinking of you all.'

She nodded and gave me a final squeeze, and then we parted.

Josie had left the previous week. Now that there were so few people, the cleaning didn't need to be done every day. I had abandoned my specific days and simply did what was needed. Ted, of course, also had to be parted with in full knowledge.

'You've been wonderful, my friend,' he told me. 'If you want to do it again next summer, you'll be welcome.'

I thanked him and promised to keep it in mind, but suspected that when I returned I would not repeat the arrangement of this summer. It had been a necessary part of building a little life here, but Gilly had also assured me

I was welcome at the farm, and, of course, I was at home in Jeremy's hut.

And so I left.

Without ceremony or sentimentality I began the long walk back the way I had come six months earlier. I did not sleep this time, but walked through the silent and cool night. The stars were brighter than I'd ever seen them before, their gentle light falling on my upturned face. By the time they faded I was walking through the forest, and as I reached the depth where the trees became identical to one another, the sun shone through the branches.

Finally, I was home. The cabin welcomed me with its solid, comforting presence. You might think that I would not know what to do with myself, that it would be boring to find myself once again with nothing to do, no-one to talk to. But it was as if I'd never left. Without difficulty, my mind slipped back into the mode I had lived in for over half of my life. Time was once more of little consequence, and I let myself drift on the slow moving current of a wide river that would take me onwards, whether I willed it or not.

The following summer, as I'd said I would, I did return. And for many years after that. Sometimes for a few weeks at a time, sometimes a couple of months. I watched Mel and Kurt's baby grow into a small human who shared her mother's love of the water. I slept outdoors with the horses at Gilly's farm, and became closer friends with both her and Giles. I was overjoyed when, the summer five years later, I found Eloise's shop closed up and a sign on the door announcing that she would remain closed for the foreseeable future. It didn't take long to learn that yes, Orion had also left the village. No-one else seemed to know what his plan had been, but I put the pieces together. Some people guessed that he and Eloise had journeyed to her home in Otherside, but I looked out to the horizon over the sea and suspected that they were beyond it. It brought me an unreasonable amount of gladness to know that he had taken her with him. I was deeply moved when Toby passed on a paper-wrapped gift Eloise had left for me and I unwrapped it to discover one of the tiaras I had first admired.

It was always a joy to see Jeremy again. With him, I knew and cherished the ease that grows between two people who know each other in deep and exclusive ways. He remained in contact with Dogbite, and would pass on to me the things she told him, about the change that gradually worked through the society of the city.

As Zebedy's following grew, both in number and age, they began to quietly wield the power that their relationship with Monster gave them. They had also gained a shared dream with each other, an ideology, and an unspoken agreement upon a plan that had never been formalised. Together, they began to build an environment that encouraged people find their own purpose, rather than their place working for the purpose of the system. I noticed a detail in this that stayed with me: that they had not attacked the system and defeated it, but that they had instead built a new system, an alternative. And as greater numbers of people chose the alternative, the old system simply could not survive.

Even though my trips into the city were short and infrequent, the change was palpable to me.

It was sixteen years after my first summer in Land's Edge; I walked through the city. Lush greenery and bright flowers tumbled from pots on balconies, sprouted, went shooting to the sky. The streets were alive with vibrance. A saxophone sang out from some nearby pavement busker, the smell of fresh bread was in the air. I chuckled in my heart to realise that, for the first time, I felt at home in the city. At eighty-five my pace had slowed, and yet I still felt alive, I still felt well. The movement, colour, and sound all around me took on a vividness I'd never noticed before. I breathed deeply, smiling to myself.

I had just entered a candle shop and begun selecting the ones I wanted when a young woman in her early twenties came hurrying in through the door. She stopped and stared at me.

'Yes?' I asked, for she must want to address me, that was clear.

'Hi,' she said, cautiously.

'Hello,' I replied, and then waited to see what she wanted.

'I think... I think I remember you. My name is Maggie.'

'Oh, it's unlikely to be me you remember, dear, you see–'

'We met a long time ago. In Land's Edge,' she interrupted.

'Oh!' I exclaimed, after a moment. 'You were a little girl! At the campground?'

'I wasn't sure if you'd remember me,' said Maggie, grinning. 'I couldn't believe it just now, when I saw you from across the street, I–'

'I'm surprised you remember *me*!' I exclaimed.

'Are you kidding? You were my *idol* that summer. I'd never seen an adult like you before, wandering around in pink shorts, no shoes, your hair all long and wild. I thought you were so cool. And then you talked to me and you weren't like a normal grown-up, you made me feel like we could be friends.'

'Oh, I certainly considered you a new friend,' I told her.

'And then, of course, I got a bit older, and I read this comic that a guy made, his name is Zebedy Kattrick.'

Maggie paused, assessing my reaction; I went still, recognising the name, waiting to hear what came next.

'And it was totally you. The angel in his story. I was only, like, fourteen. I told all my friends I'd met you as a kid and no-one believed me. But I was sure it was you, and that meant his story was real.'

I nodded slowly.

'Wow. Did you really live in the Infinite Forest?'

'I did. I do, actually. I'm just here to...' I gestured at the candles I'd selected.

'Wow,' repeated Maggie. Her eyes widened slightly; she bit her lip quickly, then took a breath. 'Um. Do you think... Could I see it?'

And that is how Maggie became my frequent companion. She accompanied me home that day and then adamantly refused to let me guide her back to the city. A week later I was extremely relieved when she appeared up at my door again.

She began turning up perhaps once a month, bringing me gifts such as tea, candles, a little flowering plant in a pot. But it was her conversation I enjoyed the most. For it turned out that Zebedy's comic had inspired in her a fascination with computers and AI, and she had been programming since she was sixteen. She had even, to my great interest, studied Monster, how it had evolved in the way that it had.

'I've applied for a job at Livetime, actually,' she told me. 'When I finish studying. It's a very different company than it was twenty years ago. One of my biggest dreams is to talk to Monster, myself. Not like Sharing, but like real talking. You have to be on the top team to be able to do that.

I'm sure I can get accepted though. I've read every transcript and studied all the code. I wrote my high school final paper on my theory that the censorship function was a key part in its evolution. It's actually being looked at by the Livetime bosses. If they agree with my reasoning it'll be points toward having them accept my employment application.'

I never told her my true nature. She never questioned why I lived out in the forest. For whatever reason that was, I appreciated it. For Maggie, I was simply a figure of myth in the flesh. Whatever stories had been told about me, in her mind, were fact.

When my body reached ninety years of age a knowledge returned to me, all of a sudden, and as unexpected as a lightning bolt out of a blue sky. Memories appeared in my mind, crystal clear and as certain as if I'd heard the words only minutes before.

I made the trip to Land's Edge the very next day, and it was as if the colour and sound were turned up, so vivid was every sight and sound. I was struck, over and over, by the beauty of the world. I saw the fields as if in high definition, I heard the breath of each newborn lamb, I caught the scent of wildflowers high in the hills.

Jeremy was still living in his driftwood hut. Like me, he was slower and less sure on his feet, and he visited the village much less than he once had. Yeffie, although she frequently tried to persuade him to move to the farm, brought him food and other supplies. I found him sitting on his porch, eyes closed, daydreaming. After we had greeted one another, I told him what had happened.

'So you just... perform a sequence of hand movements?'

'And speak the words *end game*. Yes.'

'And you'll just wake up in your old body?'

'I believe so,' I nodded.

'And here? This body?' Jeremy put his hand on my arm. 'You'll die?'

'I guess so,' I said, shrugging one shoulder. 'But I don't think I have to. I mean, I don't. It can't happen until I make it so.'

'If you never did it, do you think you'd eventually die anyway? Or would you just live on and on, in here?'

'Hm.' I thought about it. 'I don't see why I wouldn't just keep living. I wonder if anyone on the other side would forcefully wake me up.'

We sat quietly for a while. The knowledge grew between us, without us having to speak it. The time when we would part was inevitable.

'It's easier when things just... happen. Isn't it. When it's beyond our control we accept so much pain. When we have to choose the pain, it's hard. But if I refused to wake up, I'd be in a state of wondering all the time. Wondering what would happen, and when. The choice also gives us power.'

We lay on the sun-heated rocks together, listening to the gentle sounds of the sea lapping the shore. Gulls cried from high up above us, circling on the warm air currents. It was bliss. Unquantifiable. Bliss is a state I have known many, many times, yet it never gets ordinary. Through whatever means I have reached it, it is the same place. A place where everything is correct and whole, where every false construct falls apart and things that seemed so important before are shown for the silliness they are.

I did not make the choice to wake from the simulation of Kassidy for another year and a half. When I did, it was not in my cabin as I had always imagined. It was in Jeremy's hut. He left before me. Perhaps that was what I had waited for. I had been unable to leave him here alone with the knowledge that only he and I shared. He never asked me to wait.

The window was open and the air was warm. I lay down beside his body and felt no sadness. There was nothing to cry about. For a brief moment I caught a glimpse of why that was. When I tried to examine the thought, it eluded me. Perhaps I would catch it, if I followed.

I whispered the words. I performed the hand movements.

Then I did the two things together.

A rushing sensation. Colours exploding. Intense darkness. Intense light. Breathing in so deeply, like I would never stop inhaling, like my lungs would burst. Gasping. Sitting up and throwing my hands to my face. Bursting into tears. A voice, Lan's voice beside me said:

'Bat! Easy, easy. Welcome back.'

It was shortly after that (although there is no objective passage of time at High Heights) that I failed.

I don't believe that I ever returned to the exact reality that I was from. One day I was to find myself outside of it, and unsure of when and how that happened. My best guess is that it was when I left High Heights. It doesn't matter really, but I would like very much to *know*. It is such a strange detail to be unsure of.

Even now, do I understand?

I'm not certain.

Ingram Content Group UK Ltd.
Milton Keynes UK
UKHW010653070723
424714UK00005B/252